THE USBORNE
COMPUTER
DICTIONARY
FOR BEGINNERS

Anna Claybourne

Designed by Paul Greenleaf

Illustrated by Andy Burton

Photography by Howard Allman

Edited by Kamini Khanduri

Technical consultant: Richard Payne

Additional consultancy by Nick Bell

Editorial assistant: Rachael Swann

Contents

Introduction   3

Essential computer words   4

Input and output devices   6

Inside the processing unit   8

Printers   10

Types of computer   12

More types of computer   14

Peripherals   16

Computer networks   18

How computers work   20

Memory and storage   22

Software   24

Basic applications   26

Design software   28

Graphics software   30

Sound and music software   32

Games, entertainment and education   34

Programming   36

Computer problems and solutions   38

Living with computers   40

The Internet   42

The history of computers   44

The future   45

Glossary of computer slang   46

Glossary of acronyms   47

Glossary of extra words   48

Index   50

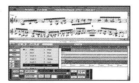

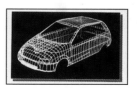

Introduction

This book is a guide to **computer jargon** - the words and phrases used to describe computers and everything related to them. Computers have developed so quickly that hundreds of new jargon words are being used to describe things that never existed before. Some computer words, like mouse, bus and virus, are normal words that have new meanings in computer jargon. Others, such as cyberspace, modem and dongle, are completely new words. There are even jargon words for "computer jargon". It can be called **computerspeak**, **technospeak**, **cyberspeak**, or **technobabble**.

Many of the words in this dictionary have been chosen to be useful to people who use a personal computer or home computer. But lots of other subjects are covered too, such as how computers work, computer history, computer culture, and what might happen in the future.

These are some of the things you can find out about in this dictionary.

Ergonomic keyboard

Silicon chip

Inkjet printer

CD-ROM drive

Digital video camera

Digital compact cassette player

Dongle

Floppy disk

Digitizer mouse

Joystick

Optical disc

Graphics tablet

Mouse

Modem

Hand-held computer game

Clip-on trackball

Using this dictionary

Instead of being arranged with all the words in alphabetical order, this dictionary is arranged by subject. For example, you can find out about computer graphics on pages 30-31, or about printers on pages 10-11.

Wherever a computer word or phrase is defined or explained, the word is printed in bold type, like this: **mouse**. If a word is explained in more detail on another page, it is printed in italic type, with an asterisk, like this: *mouse**. At the bottom of the page you will find a page number showing where to find the explanation.

To find an explanation of a particular word, first look it up in the index. The main explanation of the word is on the page shown in the index in bold type, like this: **37**. Other page numbers show other pages the word appears on.

The glossaries at the end of the book contain extra words, computer slang, and a quick guide to computer acronyms (letters that stand for words) such as RAM, ROM and VDU.

Essential computer words

A **computer** is any machine that takes in and stores **data** (information), does calculations, and gives out the results. Modern computers run on electricity and are very fast and accurate. They can work on, or **process**, all sorts of data, such as numbers, words, pictures and sounds. Many of the things computers can do are explained in this dictionary.

Input is the information fed into a computer.

Processing is the work done by a computer.

Output is the data given out by a computer.

Hardware is the machinery that makes up a computer - the solid parts, like the *keyboard**, *monitor** and *processing unit**. **Software** is the name for the instructions a computer is given so that it can do pieces of work, known as **jobs** or **tasks**. A set of instructions is called a *program**.

A **computer system** is a set of hardware and software. A **function** is something a computer can do. A computer's **functionality** is the range of things it can do. A computer that is switched on and working is said to be **up and running**, **live**, **on line** or **busy**.

A person who uses a computer system is called the **user**, or **end user**. A system that is easy to use is described as **user-friendly**. A system that is hard to use is **user-unfriendly**.

 ## Types and uses

All computers work in basically the same way, but there are lots of different types. Most of the information in this book is about **home computers**. These are small computers that can be used by one person.

A **personal computer** or **PC** is the most common kind of home computer. PCs are based on a brand of computer called the *IBM PC**, which was first made in 1981.

A *Mac** (short for Apple Macintosh) is a brand of computer which is similar to a PC, but is built differently inside. The way a computer is designed and built is called its **architecture**.

If you have a computer at home or at school, it is probably a PC or a Mac. Full-sized home computers, like the one in the big picture opposite, are called **desktop PCs**. There are also smaller PCs such as *notebooks**.

Larger computers such as *mainframes** are not home computers. They can work much faster than PCs and process more data at once. They are usually used by business people and scientists.

Many everyday machines such as washing machines and videos are **computerized** - they contain computers to help them work faster. Computers are also increasingly being used to control and organize many processes, such as storing information, communicating, and banking. This growth in the use of computers is sometimes called **digitization**. The word **digital** is used to describe a system that uses digits, or numbers, and is often used in relation to computers.

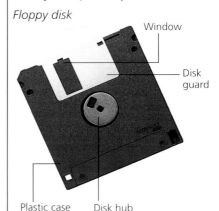 ## Storing data

While a computer is switched on, data can be stored in its *memory**. When it is switched off, most of this data is lost. To keep data safe, you have to *save** it, on a *storage device** such as the *hard disk** or a *floppy disk**. Storage devices are a vital part of any computer system.

Floppy disk

Window

Disk guard

Plastic case   Disk hub

This picture shows a personal computer with a monitor, keyboard, mouse and printer.

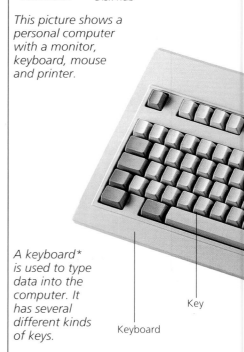

Key

Keyboard

A keyboard* is used to type data into the computer. It has several different kinds of keys.

*The space a computer takes up on a table top is called its **footprint**.*

4   *Floppy disk, 23; Hard disk, 23; IBM PC, 12; Keyboard, 6; Mac, 12; Mainframe, 14; Memory, 22; Monitor, 7; Notebook, 13; Processing unit, 8; Program, 36; Saving, 22; Storage device, 23*

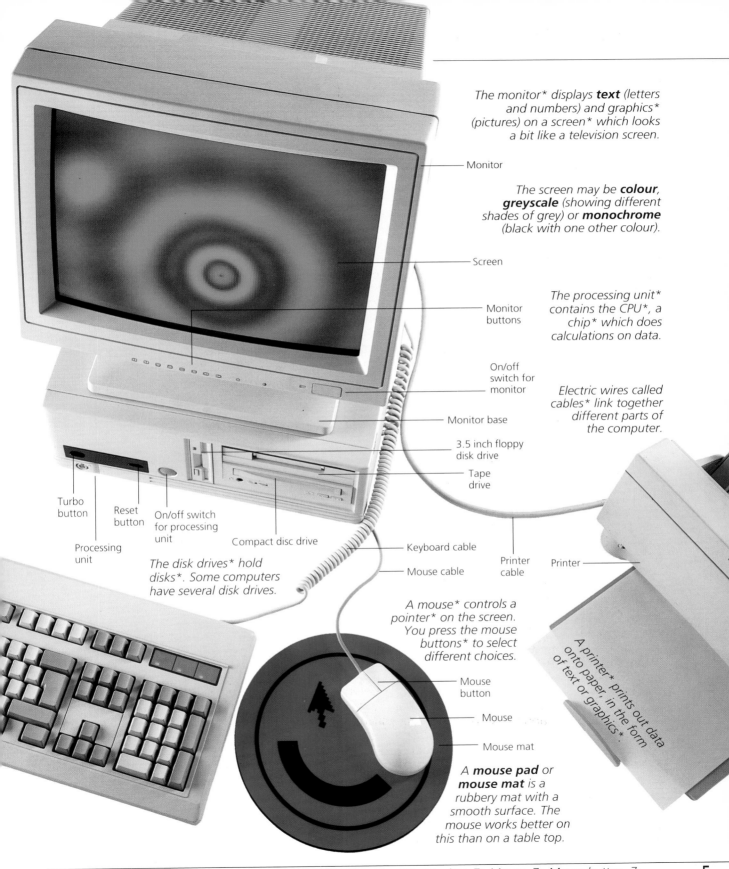

The monitor* displays **text** (letters and numbers) and graphics* (pictures) on a screen* which looks a bit like a television screen.

Monitor

The screen may be **colour**, **greyscale** (showing different shades of grey) or **monochrome** (black with one other colour).

Screen

The processing unit* contains the CPU*, a chip* which does calculations on data.

Monitor buttons

On/off switch for monitor

Electric wires called cables* link together different parts of the computer.

Monitor base

3.5 inch floppy disk drive

Tape drive

Turbo button

Reset button

On/off switch for processing unit

Processing unit

Compact disc drive

Keyboard cable

Mouse cable

Printer cable

Printer

The disk drives* hold disks*. Some computers have several disk drives.

A mouse* controls a pointer* on the screen. You press the mouse buttons* to select different choices.

A printer* prints out data onto paper, in the form of text or graphics*.

Mouse button

Mouse

Mouse mat

A **mouse pad** or **mouse mat** is a rubbery mat with a smooth surface. The mouse works better on this than on a table top.

*Cable, 17; Chip, 21; CPU, 9; Disk, 23; Disk drive, 23; Graphics, 30; Monitor, 7; Mouse, 7; Mouse button, 7; Pointer, 7; Printer, 10; Processing unit, 8; Screen, 7

Input and output devices

A computer does all its processing in numbers. For people to communicate, or **interact**, with a computer, these numbers have to be translated into a language they can understand. **Input devices**, such as the keyboard, translate data from the user and carry it, or **input** it, into the computer. **Output devices**, such as the monitor, translate the results and send, or **output**, them back to the user. The keyboard, mouse and monitor are the basic input and output devices on most *PCs**, but there are many other kinds.

Input devices can carry all kinds of data into computers, such as *text**, *sound** and pictures. For example, a **barcode reader**, or **barcode scanner**, is used in shops to read **barcodes** (price labels made up of black and white stripes) and send the price back to a computer in the till.

Barcode reader

Output devices can give you all sorts of output, such as *graphics**, *printouts** and public messages. For example, **computerized public displays** and **dot matrix indicators** show moving messages in shops or at stations and airports. The messages are *programmed** into a computer which is linked to the display.

Computerized public display

The keyboard

The **keyboard** usually has **alphanumeric** (letter and number) **keys** on it, arranged in the same pattern as on a typewriter (called the **QWERTY** pattern). There are also extra keys, called dedicated keys (see below) and function keys (see right). There are different kinds of keyboards on many *computerized** machines, such as the *keypad** on a TV remote control, and the *control panel** on a microwave oven. You may also see **touch-sensitive keyboards** with panels on a flat surface instead of raised keys.

- **Function keys** These can be *programmed** to do special jobs.
- **Numeric keypad** A pad with numbers arranged like those on a calculator, to make it easy to use.
- **Cursor control keys** Keys that move a cursor (see facing page).
- **Space bar** Puts a space on the screen between **characters** (letters, numbers and symbols).
- **PAGE UP** and **PAGE DOWN keys** These let you **scroll**, or move your *document**, up and down on the screen to look at different parts of it.
- **Keyboard feet** Little pegs under the keyboard. They tilt the keyboard towards you so it is more comfortable to use.

A typical computer keyboard

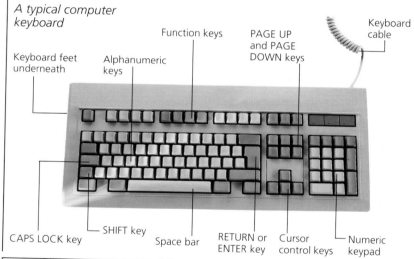

Keyboard feet underneath
Alphanumeric keys
Function keys
PAGE UP and PAGE DOWN keys
Keyboard cable
CAPS LOCK key
SHIFT key
Space bar
RETURN or ENTER key
Cursor control keys
Numeric keypad

Dedicated keys

Dedicated keys have a word or symbol on them. They give the computer a particular instruction.

The **RETURN** or **ENTER** key (sometimes an arrow symbol) is pressed at the end of an instruction to tell the computer to carry it out.

RETURN

ENTER

*Some keys are used to change the function of other keys. For example, you press **SHIFT** and the 'e' key to get a capital E.*

***Toggle keys**, such as **CAPS LOCK** and **INSERT**, are pressed once to start working, and again to go back to normal.*

SHIFT

CONTROL

CAPS LOCK

INSERT

*Computerized, 4; Control panel, 15; Document, 25; Graphics, 30; Keypad, 27; PC, 4, 12; Printout, 10; Programming, 36; Sound, 32; Text, 5

The mouse

A **mouse** (plural: **mouses** or **mice**) moves a **pointer** on the screen. You use a mouse by moving it across a *mouse pad**. You **select** an instruction from the screen by **clicking** (pressing and releasing) or **double clicking** (pressing twice) on a **mouse button**. **Clicking and dragging** means holding down a button as you move the mouse.

An **ergonomic mouse** (which can be right-handed or left-handed) is curved to fit your hand. Most mouses are linked to the computer by a *cable** or **tail**. Mouses without tails are called **cordless** or **tail-less mouses**. These send information back to the

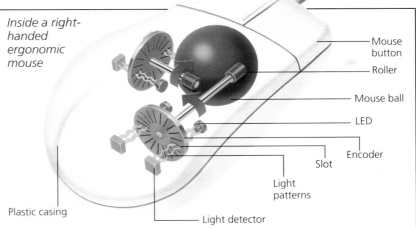

Inside a right-handed ergonomic mouse

Mouse button
Roller
Mouse ball
LED
Encoder
Slot
Light patterns
Plastic casing
Light detector

computer in the form of invisible infra-red light signals.

When you move a mouse, a rubber **mouse ball** inside rolls across the pad. The ball turns two **rollers**, and they turn wheels called **encoders**. Tiny

lights called **LEDs** (**Light-Emitting Diodes**) shine light through slots in the encoders to make light patterns. These are sensed by **light detectors** and turned into information about how the mouse has moved.

The monitor

The **monitor** or **VDU** (**Visual Display Unit**) shows you data on a **screen** and displays different options. There are two main kinds of monitor. *Liquid Crystal Display** (LCD) monitors are often used with *notebooks**. **CRT** (**Cathode Ray Tube**) **monitors** are large and look like televisions. They usually have **graphics adaptors** - devices which give a monitor high-quality *graphics**. There are two main types of graphics adaptor: **VGA** (**Video Graphics Array**) or **SVGA** (**Super Video Graphics Array**).

The picture on a monitor's screen is called an **image**. A monitor's **resolution** means the sharpness of its image. A **high resolution** image is made up of small dots and is very clear and sharp. A **low resolution** image is made up of larger dots, and does not show such clear and realistic pictures.

• The resolution depends on the number of dots, or **pixels** (short for **picture elements**) that make up the screen. A modern SVGA monitor has over a million pixels.
• **Glare** means the screen reflects light and damages your eyes. Some screens have an **anti-glare filter** to reduce glare.
• The monitor gives out a small amount of harmful **radiation**. **Low-radiation** or **low-rad**

monitors give out less radiation.
• A **cursor** shows where the next character (see facing page) you type will appear.
• A **degauss button** gets rid of static electricity, which stops the screen from working properly.
• **Brightness** and **contrast buttons** let you alter the image.
• **Size controls** and **centre controls** move and stretch the image on the screen.

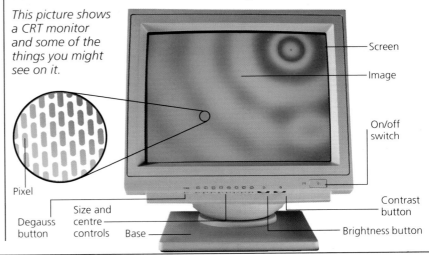

This picture shows a CRT monitor and some of the things you might see on it.

Screen
Image
On/off switch
Contrast button
Brightness button
Pixel
Degauss button
Size and centre controls
Base

Inside the processing unit

The **processing unit** is the main part of a computer, where data is stored and processed. It is also called the **systems unit**, and sometimes just the **computer** or even the **hard disk** (although the *hard disk** is just one part of it). It is made up of *chips** and several other parts inside a strong *case**.

The chips and other devices are arranged on plastic boards called **PCBs (Printed Circuit Boards)**. The main PCB is called the **motherboard** or **mainboard**, and smaller PCBs joined onto it are called **daughterboards** or **cards**. Printed pathways, called **tracks**, make up **electrical circuits**, which carry data around the computer.

Tracks are usually arranged in groups called *buses**. Data travels along the buses from one chip to another. Buses contain slots called **expansion slots**. You can fit extra PCBs called **expansion cards** into these to improve your *PC's** performance - for example, to give it better *sound** or *graphics**.

On the front

There are several buttons on the front of the processing unit. The **on/off switch** starts your computer working (known as **booting up**). You can boot up again (**reboot**), without switching off completely, by pressing the **reset button**. The **turbo button** changes the clock speed (see facing page). Lights called **LED indicators** show that the computer is on, and a **loudspeaker** makes sounds.

The *hard disk drive** fits into spare space inside the *case**. *Floppy disk drives** and *CD-ROM drives** fit into **drive bays** in the front of the processing unit.

Ports

A **port**, or **I/O port** (short for **Input/Output port**) is a socket in the back of the processing unit that allows you to connect *input and output devices** to it. On a *PC** there are usually two kinds of port: *parallel ports** and *serial ports**. Some ports are for specific uses, such as the **mouse port** and the **keyboard port**.

This photo shows what the processing unit really looks like inside.

This picture shows some of the parts inside the processing unit more clearly.

Interfaces

An **interface** is an electrical circuit which controls and adapts the signals passing between the processing unit and another piece of *hardware**. There are several types of interface. Sometimes another circuit called a **PIA (Peripheral Interface Adaptor)** is also needed to link pieces of hardware together.

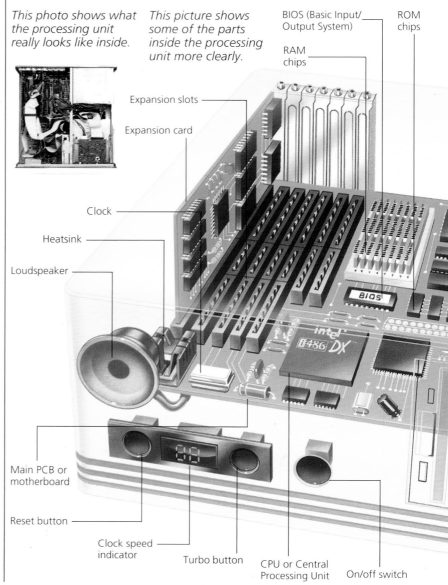

Expansion slots

Expansion card

Clock

Heatsink

Loudspeaker

Main PCB or motherboard

Reset button

Clock speed indicator

Turbo button

CPU or Central Processing Unit

On/off switch

BIOS (Basic Input/Output System)

ROM chips

RAM chips

*Bus, 20; Case, 12; CD-ROM drive, 35; Chip, 21; Floppy disk drive, 23; Graphics, 30; Hard disk, 23; Hard disk drive, 23; Hardware, 4; Input and output devices, 6; Parallel and serial ports, 17; PC, 4, 12; Sound, 32

ROM and RAM

A computer has two main kinds of *memory**. *ROM** stores the instructions that tell the computer how to start working. The **BIOS** (**Basic Input/Output System**) is usually part of ROM and contains instructions for running the *input and output devices**. *RAM** stores data while the computer is working on it, but loses most of this data when you switch the computer off.

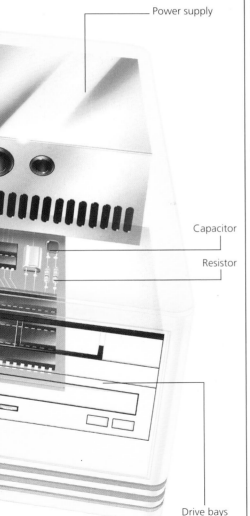

Power supply

Capacitor

Resistor

Drive bays

The CPU

The **Central Processing Unit** or **CPU** (also called the **processor** or **microprocessor**) is the "brain" of a computer. It is a large *chip** (or group of chips) that controls all the computer's calculations, or **operations**.

Diagram of the main parts of a CPU chip

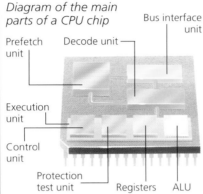

Bus interface unit

Prefetch unit

Decode unit

Execution unit

Control unit

Protection test unit

Registers

ALU

Different CPUs have different kinds of structure, or *architecture**, but they all work in a similar way. This list explains what the main parts of a CPU do.
- **Bus interface unit** fetches instructions from *RAM** and passes them to the prefetch unit.
- **Prefetch unit** keeps the instructions in a queue, ready to pass on to the decode unit.
- **Decode unit** translates each instruction so that it is ready to be processed.
- **Execution unit** is the part that does the actual processing. It has four main sections:
- **Control unit** sends instructions to other parts of the execution unit, for example to collect data, do calculations and send the results to RAM.
- **Protection test unit** checks for **errors** (mistakes).
- **Registers** hold pieces of data that are being calculated.
- **Arithmetic Logic Unit** (**ALU**) performs the calculations.

Power and speed

Computers work at various speeds, depending on the individual computer's clock speed and processing power.

The **clock** is a device that sends electrical signals called **pulses** around the computer. On each pulse, or **clock cycle**, the computer does one calculation. A *PC** has a **clock speed** (or **clock rate**) of up to 100 million **clock cycles per second** (100 **megahertz**). Some PCs have a lit-up **clock speed indicator** on the front.

Processing power is the speed at which the CPU works. The speed depends on the kind of CPU a computer has. Most PCs have *Intel** CPUs, such as the 286, 386, 486 and Pentium Processor™. *Macs** and many larger computers use different kinds of CPU.

Components

A processing unit contains many electronic parts, or **components**. These include the **power supply**, which converts electricity from the mains supply into the right voltage for the computer, and **resistors** and **capacitors** which control the flow of electricity around the circuits. A **heatsink** is a piece of metal attached to a chip. It stops the chip from getting too hot, which can stop it from working.

Capacitor

Heatsink

Resistor

---

*Architecture, 4; Chip, 21; Input and output devices, 6; Intel, 12; Mac, 12; Memory, 22; PC, 4, 12; RAM and ROM, 22

Printers

Printers are *output devices** that print out data, usually onto paper. A piece of printed *output** is called a **printout** or **hard copy**. (**Soft copy** is data held in an electronic form.)

There are several kinds of printers with different ways of working. Some can only print *text**; others can print *graphics** too. **Black and white printers** are more common, while **colour printers** are more expensive and often slower. Printers work at various speeds. **Character printers** (or **serial printers**) print one *character** at a time. **Line printers** print one line at a time and **page printers** print a page at a time.

Printers are either impact or non-impact. **Impact printers** print by hitting an inked **printer ribbon** against the paper. **Non-impact printers** squirt or press ink (or powdered ink called **toner**) onto the paper. Most printers use **ink cartridges** or **toner cartridges** which can be replaced when they run out.

Printed images are usually made up of thousands of tiny dots. The smaller the dots, the sharper and clearer the printout. The sharpness of the printout is called the **print resolution**.

Sending files

When you want to print a *file** you have to **send** it to a printer. Most computers are linked to a printer by a **printer** *cable**. Some *dedicated word processors** have a **built-in printer**.

A *program** in your computer, called a **printer driver**, converts your file into instructions for the printer. A **print spooler** is a program that organizes and arranges any files that are waiting to be printed.

Types of printer

Most types of printer have the same basic mechanism. A moving **print head** prints from side to side across the paper. The paper is held by a large roller called a **platen** and some smaller rollers inside. A **carriage return** *function** moves the paper up for each new line. Laser printers (see facing page) work differently.

Parts of a dot matrix printer

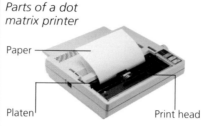

Paper

Platen

Print head

Some different types of printer

Inkjet printer

Laser printer

Colour printer

• **Dot matrix printers** are impact printers. They have a group, or **matrix**, of tiny **printing pins** on the print head. As the print head moves, the pins move forward in different patterns, pressing the printer ribbon onto the paper.

Print head of a dot matrix printer

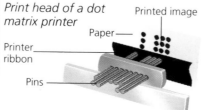

Printed image

Paper

Printer ribbon

Pins

• **Daisywheel printers** have a large **daisywheel** on the print head, with raised *characters** on "**petals**" around the edge. The wheel spins very quickly, while a **hammer** pushes the petals against the ribbon and onto the paper one at a time.

Part of a daisywheel print head

Daisywheel

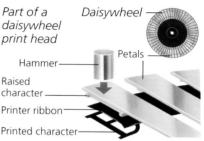

Hammer

Petals

Raised character

Printer ribbon

Printed character

• **Inkjet** or **bubblejet printers** make up characters out of lots of tiny ink droplets. The print head contains up to 50 **ink chambers**. When each chamber is heated, a drop of ink boils and bursts out of a **nozzle** onto the paper.

Enlarged cross-section of an ink chamber

Ink

Paper

Nozzle

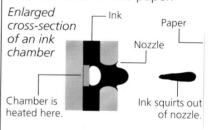

Chamber is heated here.

Ink squirts out of nozzle.

• **Colour printers** usually use a process called **four-colour printing**. Four colours - **black**, **yellow**, **cyan** (a kind of turquoise) and **magenta** (bright pink) - are printed one at a time. Combinations of these colours make full-colour pictures. Colour printers are usually dot matrix or inkjet printers with four separate print heads, one for each colour. Some colour printers use **three-colour printing** and have only three colours (not black). They make a kind of black, called **registration black**, by combining all three colours.

Cable, 17; Character, 6; Dedicated word processor, 15; File, 25; Function, 4; Graphics, 30; Output, 4; Output devices, 6; Program, 36; Text, 5

Laser printers

Laser printers are the fastest and sharpest printers. They use a **laser beam** (an intense beam of light) to make dots of invisible electrical power, or charge, on a roller called a **drum**. Toner (see facing page) sticks to the dots of charge, and the toner-covered drum is then pressed against the paper. The **fusing system** fixes the toner permanently.

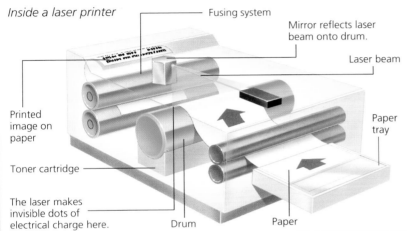

Inside a laser printer

- Fusing system
- Mirror reflects laser beam onto drum.
- Laser beam
- Paper tray
- Paper
- Drum
- The laser makes invisible dots of electrical charge here.
- Toner cartridge
- Printed image on paper

Printer memory

Like a computer, a printer has two kinds of *memory** - **printer ROM**, which holds instructions that make the printer work, and **printer RAM**, which stores data while the printer is switched on.

Printers can work in two ways. The first way is to store instructions, called **bitmaps**, for each *character**. Most printers have bitmaps for a few basic character styles (called *fonts** or *typefaces**) stored in ROM. More bitmaps can be added, or *downloaded**, and held in RAM.

The second way is for the computer to use a **Page Description Language** (PDL) such as **PostScript**. A PDL lets you print detailed *graphics**. It gives the printer exact instructions describing how to draw the image on the page. Characters are described by sets of instructions called **outlines**.

Printer paper

Several kinds of paper are made specially for computer printers. **Continuous stationery** is a long strip of sheets joined together. It can be either **fanfold paper** (also called **accordion fold** or **concertina fold**) or **roll paper** (also called **printer roll**). Single pieces of paper are called **cut sheet paper**. Printers move, or **feed**, the paper upwards as they print. **Line feed** moves the paper line by line, and **form feed** moves it a page at a time. **Reverse feed** can move the paper backwards.

Fanfold paper

Roll paper

Printer words

- **cps (characters per second)** Describes printing speed. Fast dot matrix printers print at 150cps.
- **ppm (pages per minute)** A measure of fast speeds. Some laser printers print up to 20ppm.
- **dpi (dots per inch)** The number of dots that make up an inch of a printed image. The higher the dpi, the sharper the image.
- **Print server** or **printer server** A computer that holds *files** that are waiting to be printed, and stores them on its *hard disk** in a **print queue**. Print servers are used on *networks** where users share a printer (**print sharing**).
- **Image quality** The sharpness of a printout, measured in dpi. **NLQ (Near Letter Quality)** and **letter quality** are very sharp. Quicker **draft quality** is used when printouts don't have to look so good.
- **Memory buffer** A part of the printer's *RAM** that stores data that is waiting to be printed.
- **Consumables** Things that get used up, like paper, toner and printer ribbon (see facing page).
- **Bi-directional printing** This means the print head (see facing page) can print either from left to right or from right to left. **Logic-seeking print heads** save time by starting the next line at the side nearest to their last position.
- **Tractor** This feeds a supply of continuous stationery into the printer. Toothed wheels called **sprockets** hold the paper in the right place.

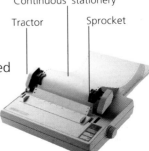

- Continuous stationery
- Tractor
- Sprocket

*Character, 6; Downloading, 19; File, 25; Font, 26; Graphics, 30; Hard disk, 23; Memory, 22; Network, 18, 42; RAM and ROM, 22; Typeface, 26

11

Types of computer

There are thousands of types of computer, from tiny ones you can carry around, to large, complicated systems with hundreds of users.

The first computers were very big, because they contained lots of large parts. Small computers appeared when the *chip** was invented in the 1960s. A **personal computer**, or **PC**, is a small computer which has its own *processing unit**, *monitor** and *keyboard** and is usually used by one person.

Early PCs were called **microcomputers** or **micros**, because they were smaller than the computers that had existed before. One of the first was the *Altair**, made in 1971. In the 1980s, micros such as the **ZX81**, the **ZX Spectrum**, the **Vic 20**, the **Commodore 64** and the **BBC Computer** became very popular, and some people still use them. Most of these computers have their processing unit under the keyboard, and use a television as a monitor.

ZX Spectrum

People started using the name "PC" after the *IBM** **Personal Computer** was introduced in 1981. Soon other companies began making similar computers (known as **IBM clones**), and these started to be called PCs too. Now, **IBM-compatible** means a PC that works like an IBM PC, and can use the same pieces of *software**.

PCs come in various sizes and have different features. A list of these features is called a **specification** or **spec**.

Macs

A **Mac** (short for **Apple Macintosh**) is a kind of computer which is similar to IBM PCs and IBM clones (see left), but which has a different kind of *architecture**. A company called **Apple Computer** started making Macs in 1984. Macs are not IBM-compatible (see left), so they need different *software**. However, *IBM** and Apple have worked together to make the **Power PC** and the **Power Mac**, which can **emulate** (imitate) each other and so can use the same software.

Apple Macintosh computer

Cases

Modern PCs are made in various shapes. The box containing the *processing unit** is called the **case** or **chassis**. A flat case is called a **desktop case**.

Desktop case

A vertical case is called a **tower**. Towers can usually hold several *disk drives**. There are three main sizes of tower.

Mini tower   **Midi tower**   **Full tower**

Chip numbers

Many PCs are labelled "**Intel Inside**", which means they use a *CPU** *chip** made by a company called **Intel**. A name such as **486** (short for **Intel 80486**) describes the type of Intel chip used. The higher the number, or **generation**, the more powerful the chip.

- **286** or **AT** The first well-known Intel chip used in PCs.
- **386SX** and **386DX** These chips have a bigger *bus** than the 286.
- **486SX** Has an internal cache (a kind of extra *memory**).
- **486DX** Has an internal cache and a *co-processor** (an extra processing chip).
- **486DX2** and **486DX4** Have faster *processing speeds** than the 486DX.
- **Pentium™ Processor** The next generation in the Intel family of chips. Has two caches and an extra-wide 64-bit bus.

Macs use different chips, called the **68020**, **68030**, and **68040**, made by a company called **Motorola**.

The Power PC and Power Mac use a special **Power PC chip**.

Upgrading

Upgrading means improving a PC's performance. A PC's **upgradability** means the extent to which it can be upgraded. A **fully upgradable** PC can have nearly all its parts replaced or added to. For example, a PC with **expandable RAM** can have more *RAM** *chips** added. A **user-removable** *CPU** can be taken out so a new one can be plugged in. **Zero Insertion Force** (**ZIF**) **sockets** are sockets inside the *processing unit** that are easy to plug chips into, so you can upgrade your own computer.

Shrinking PCs

Portable _PCs_* can be closed up like a briefcase and carried around. The first portables (called **luggables** or **carry-and-park portables**) were quite heavy and had to be plugged in. Now, most portables are **notebooks**, also called **laptops** or **work-on-the-go portables**, which don't have to be plugged in. They have **NiCad** (**Nickel Cadmium**) or **NiMH** (**Nickel Metal Hydride**) rechargeable batteries, or **battery packs**.

Some notebooks can be plugged into a **docking station**, a base which turns the notebook into _desktop PC_*, with a full-sized _CRT monitor_* and space for extra _expansion cards_*.

Instead of a _mouse_*, note-books often have a **trackball** (also called a **trackerball** or **thumball**) built into the _keyboard_*. You roll the ball with your hand to move a _pointer_* on the screen. Sometimes notebooks have a **clip-on** or **snap-on trackball** instead, which fits on the side of the keyboard, or a **pen mouse** or **ballpoint mouse**, a mouse shaped like a pen, with the ball in its tip.

Clip-on trackball

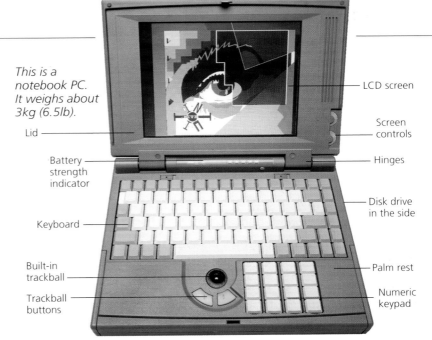

This is a notebook PC. It weighs about 3kg (6.5lb).

- Lid
- Battery strength indicator
- Keyboard
- Built-in trackball
- Trackball buttons
- LCD screen
- Screen controls
- Hinges
- Disk drive in the side
- Palm rest
- Numeric keypad

• The flat screen is usually an **LCD** (**Liquid Crystal Display**) **screen**, which works by shining light through a special liquid. **Dual scan LCD screens** replace, or **refresh**, the light on the screen twice as fast as normal or **standard passive LCD screens**.
• **TFT** (**Thin Film Transistor**) screens are a kind of flat screen. They are brighter than LCD screens and show more colours.
• A **detachable lid** allows the screen to be swapped for a newer, better one.
• **External _ports_***, or **outlets**, such as a keyboard port, link the notebook to full-size _input and output devices_*.
• Some notebooks have **dual batteries**, so you can change, or **hot swap**, to a second battery when the first runs out. Meanwhile, a **RAM capacitor** keeps the notebook running.
• A **mains adaptor** lets a notebook use the mains electricity supply. An **autosensing power supply** can convert electricity from any mains socket.
• If you leave the notebook on, **auto suspend** makes it use less power, or **power down**. **Auto resume** makes it start working again when you press a key or move the mouse.
• A notebook can use a small internal or portable _modem_* for connecting to a _network_*.

Pocket PCs

Palmtops, also called **sub-notebooks** or **hand-held PCs**, are tiny _PCs_*, even smaller than notebooks (see above). Some of them can run complicated _programs_*, such as _spreadsheets_*, but they do not have much _memory_*. They can weigh less than 400g (14oz).

Personal organizers or **electronic diaries** are tiny computers for storing notes, reminders and addresses. Some have **pen-based input** - you write straight onto the screen and the computer recognizes your writing with a **character recognition program**. You can also store data on tiny **memory cards** to keep it safe.

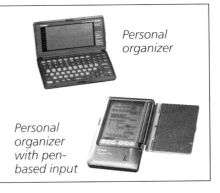

Personal organizer

Personal organizer with pen-based input

---

*CRT monitor, 7; Desktop PC, 4; Expansion card, 8; Input and output devices, 6; Keyboard, 6; Memory, 22; Modem, 19; Mouse, 7; Network, 18, 42; PC, 4, 12; Pointer, 7; Port, 8; Program, 36; Spreadsheet, 27

More types of computer

 ## Big computers

The first computers were bigger than modern ones. In the mid-1800s, a scientist called **Charles Babbage** designed an early computer, called the *Analytical Engine**, but it was too large for him to build. The first electronic computer, *ENIAC**, built in 1945, was so big it took up an area as big as ten large cars.

Charles Babbage

Today, the biggest computers are **mainframes**, which are used to process very large amounts of data (called **number crunching**). They have a powerful *processing unit**, linked to many **terminals**. A terminal has a *monitor** and a *keyboard** for a user to work at. This is called **centralized** computing. The processing unit is very sensitive and must be kept at the right temperature. It is often stored at a different place from the terminals, which are linked to it by a *network**. This is called **remote processing**.

Mainframes work by **timesharing**. This means that the users (called *end users** or **multiple users**) can all share the processing unit without interfering with each other's work. The computer appears to be doing lots of jobs at once. In fact, it quickly swaps between the different jobs. This is called **multitasking**. The mainframe in a large company is run by the **Data Processing (DP) department** or the **Information Technology (IT) department**.

Minicomputers are small mainframes. **Supercomputers** are very powerful computers used to do extremely complicated calculations.

 ## Parallel jobs

Parallel computing or **parallel processing** means computing with a large number of *CPU** *chips** at the same time. Parallel computing is often used for jobs that deal with huge amounts of data (called **knowledge-based projects**), such as working out weather forecasts. Parallel computers usually process groups, or **arrays**, of pieces of data (called **data elements**). They need a special kind of *programming**, called **parallel programming** or **concurrent programming**.

SIMD (Single Instruction Multiple Data) parallel processing means the CPUs all do the same job on lots of data. **MIMD (Multiple Instruction Multiple Data)** means the different CPUs can do different jobs at the same time.

Data processing

A data processing department (see above) often has several sections, all connected to a mainframe (see above).

*In the **operations section**, computer operators, data entry workers or keyboardists input* data into the mainframe.*

*Data is stored in a **data library**, usually on large tape cartridges*.*

*At the **information section** or **help desk, support staff** give other users advice about how to use the system.*

*Technicians and **technical support staff** look after computer equipment and solve the more difficult software* problems.*

*In the **applications section, systems analysts** design new programs* and programmers* write them.*

*Mainframes often have a **print department**. Documents* are printed there, collected and returned to the users.*

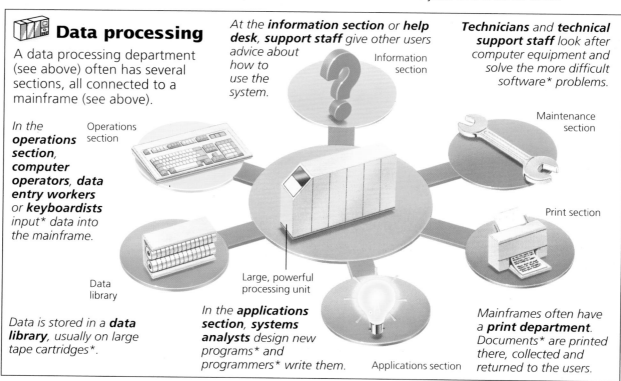

Information section

Maintenance section

Print section

Operations section

Data library

Large, powerful processing unit

Applications section

*Analytical Engine, 44; Chip, 21; CPU, 9; Document, 25; End user, 4; ENIAC, 44; Input, 6; Keyboard, 6; Monitor, 7; Network, 18, 42; Processing unit, 8; Program(ming), 36; Software, 4, 24; Tape cartridge, 23

Workstations

Workstation can mean the desk where you use your computer. But it also means a powerful type of computer. These workstations have their own *processing units** and are usually used by one person, but they can be linked together so that their power can be shared by many users across a *network**. They are often used for *computer-aided design** and can sometimes have very large, high-quality flat screens.

A type of workstation computer

Flat screen

Case

 ## Dedication

Dedicated or **special-purpose computers** are built to do just one job. **Dedicated word processors** and **electronic typewriters** are computers made just for writing, and *games computers** are just for playing games. Dedicated computers are good at what they do, but they often can't run new *programs**, so they go out of date quickly.

General-purpose computers are computers that aren't dedicated.

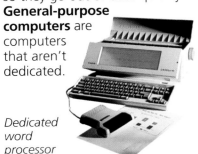

Dedicated word processor

 ## Other uses

These are some of the many ways computers are used in different areas of life.

• Lots of household items, such as video recorders and microwave ovens, are *computerized**. You *input** instructions by pressing buttons on a **control panel**. Your instructions are really a kind of short *program**.

Microwave oven　　　Control panel

• In shops, **cashless payment** or **EFTPOS (Electronic Funds Transfer at Point Of Sale) systems** let you pay for goods using a card. A computer reads details from a **magnetic strip** on your card, and uses *network** links to check the details with your bank's computer. Many shops also have **computerized checkouts**. Each item in the shop has a **UPC** (**Unique Product Code**). A computer reads the code and shows the price. It also keeps a record of all the things that are sold.

• **CAM** (**Computer-Aided Manufacturing**), or **factory automation**, uses computers to control **robots** - machines that can do work instead of humans. **Hard automation** means the machines are dedicated (see left) and can do only one task. More complicated robots can be programmed to do a variety of different jobs. Some have **vision systems** and can "see" their work using a camera. **Guided vehicle systems** are mobile robots that can find their way around a factory.

• To get into museums or underground stations, you often need a **computer-coded ticket**. This has a magnetic strip (see left) on the back containing coded information. You put the ticket into a special gate, where a computer reads the strip and opens the gate.

Computer-coded ticket

TOM'S TRAVEL & TRANSPORT
Valid for 1 journey

Not transferable

Magnetic strip

• **Touchscreens** are often used in museums and information centres. You can choose which information to see on the screen by pressing different parts of it.

• **Technological warfare** means using computers to make weapons more deadly. Modern missiles have computerized **electronic guidance systems** so that they can find their targets.

• **Computer-assisted therapy** means using computers to help people. For example, there is a *computer game** which teaches deaf children to pronounce words.

• **CAT** (**Computerized Axial Tomography**) **scanners** in hospitals use computers to make colour 3-D X-rays, or **CAT scans.** These show a very clear picture of the inside of parts of the body.

CAT scan of a hand

---

*Computer-aided design, 29; Computerized, 4; Games computer, 34; Input, 6; Network, 18, 42; Processing unit, 8; Program, 36

Peripherals

In computing, the word **peripheral** really means any piece of *hardware** apart from the computer's actual *processing unit**. But it is also used to mean an extra piece of hardware which you add to your *computer system** to do a particular job, such as extra *input and output devices**. A number of peripherals sold together is called a **kit** or a **bundle** - for example, you can buy a *multimedia bundle**, containing everything you need to run *multimedia** *software**.

 ## Game control

Joysticks are peripherals used to play computer *games**. A joystick has a steering stick set into a base, with **fire buttons** for shooting. An **autofire button** lets you fire continuously, without pressing again and again. Suction feet hold the joystick firmly to the table.

A **control pad** is like a joystick, but has no stick, only buttons.

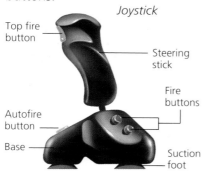

Joystick

Top fire button

Steering stick

Fire buttons

Autofire button

Base

Suction foot

Lots of computer games involve flying an aircraft or a spacecraft. A **flightstick** is a special joystick made for flying games. A **flight yoke** is a larger device with a kind of steering wheel which you hold with both hands. A **flight console** is even bigger, and consists of a flight yoke with pedals.

 ## Pointing devices

A type of peripheral called a **pointing device** allows you to point at and select options on the screen. An ordinary *mouse** is the most common kind, but there are lots of others. For example, a **long-distance mouse** is used to move a *pointer** on a large screen for showing something to an audience. Its long cable lets you stand away from the screen.

Some pointing devices are used for drawing and writing on the screen. A **graphics tablet** is a flat pad which you can write or draw on. The marks you make appear on the screen.

Long-distance mouse

Graphics tablet

Scanners

A **scanner** or **image scanner** is a machine used to copy an image from paper into a computer. This is called **scanning in**. A device called a **scan head** inside the scanner bounces light off the image. The patterns of light are collected by **Charge Coupled Devices** (**CCDs**). These send information about the image to the computer, which then recreates the image on the screen.

Most scanners can do **colour scans**, **monochrome** or **mono scans** (black and white), or **halftone scans** (different shades of grey).
- There are several kinds of **flatbed scanners.** You usually put the image on a piece of glass called a **scanner window**, and the scan head slowly moves across it.

Flatbed scanner

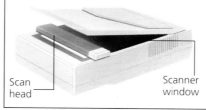

Scan head

Scanner window

- A **hand scanner** is useful for small images. You drag, or **track**, it slowly across the image. A special **scan mat** or **track pad** can be used to hold the image still.

Hand scanner

Image

- A **drum scanner** produces high-quality scans. The image is taped onto a cylinder or **drum**. The drum spins round very quickly while a scan head scans the image.
- **Mark scanners** are used to read questionnaires and multiple choice exam papers. The scanner reads which boxes have been ticked and the computer sorts out the results.
- **Optical Character Recognition** (**OCR**) **scanners** can scan written and printed *text**. A computer *program** recognizes the letters by **matrix matching** (comparing each letter shape to its own store of letters) or by **feature extraction** (analyzing the parts of each shape).

**Computer system, 4; Games, 34; Hardware, 4; Input and output devices, 6; Mouse, 7; Multimedia, 35; Multimedia bundle, 35; Pointer, 7; Processing unit, 8; Program, 36; Software, 4, 24; Text, 5*

Carrying data

Cables, **leads** or **wires** link peripherals to your computer. **Connectors** on the ends of the cables plug into *ports** in the back of the *processing unit**, and into sockets in the peripherals they are connected to. Ports and cables work in two main ways - **serial transmission** and **parallel transmission**. Parallel transmission can carry more data at a time.

Serial ports and **serial cables** can only carry, or **transmit**, one *bit** of data at a time. They are often used for *mouses** and *modems**, which do not send much data at a time. An **RS-232 port** is a common kind of serial port.

A serial cable has two **data wires**, or **data lines**, for carrying data - one in each direction - and extra wires which carry other signals to control the transmission of the data.

Serial cable

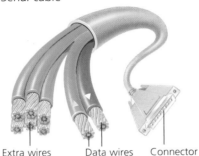

Extra wires   Data wires   Connector

Parallel ports (often called **printer ports**) and **parallel cables** can transmit a whole *byte** (eight bits) of data at a time, along eight parallel wires

inside the cable. They are usually used for *printers** and plotters (see below) which need to receive a lot of data.

A parallel cable has eight data wires in each direction.

Parallel cable

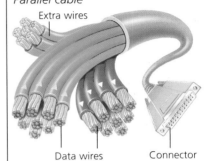

Extra wires

Data wires   Connector

Data travelling in a cable can be damaged by **interference** caused by electricity from somewhere else. The longer a cable is, the worse the interference.

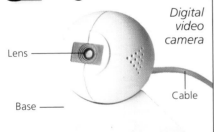 ## Digital cameras

Digital video camera

Lens

Base

Cable

Ordinary cameras convert light into an image on a piece of film. **Digital cameras** convert light into *binary** data - information stored in a code made up of zeros and ones. A digital camera can be plugged into a *PC**, in order to see the image on the screen.

Digital video cameras are used to *input** moving pictures in the same way. They are used for **video conferencing** or **teleconferencing**, where several people are linked together on a *network** and can

see each other talking on their computer screens. Video conferencing can use **full motion** (high-quality) **video**, or **freeze frame video**, which is poorer quality but easier to send across a network.

Digital cameras are also used to input images which can be processed by a computer to make *computer art**.

Home help

Home automation means using computers to control things such as light switches and heating. A peripheral called a **butler in a box** can be linked to a computer. It "hears" spoken instructions and sends signals to automatic devices around the house. It is very useful for disabled people.

Butler in a box

Plotters

A **plotter** is an *output device** for making complex, detailed drawings, such as maps and architects' plans, which are too big for a normal *printer**.

Pen plotters draw with **plotter pens**, which are held by a *robot** arm inside the plotter. There are **drafting pens** for rough drawings, or high-quality fibre-tips for final copies. The **line quality** means the thinness and clearness of the pen's line.

Inkjet plotters work just like *inkjet printers**.

A free-standing inkjet plotter

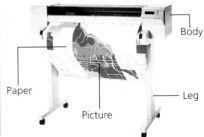

Body

Paper

Picture

Leg

---

*Binary, 20; Bit, 20; Byte, 20; Computer art, 31; Inkjet printer, 10; Input, 6; Modem, 19; Mouse, 7; Network, 18, 42; Output device, 6; PC, 4, 12; Port, 8; Printer, 10; Processing unit, 8; Robot, 15

Computer networks

Networks link computers together so they can send information to each other. On a network, you can send data to another computer in the same building, in a different town or on the other side of the world. You can send *text**, *graphics**, *sound** or any other kind of *computerized** information.

Sending data in this way is called **telecommunications** or **datacommunications**. This is often shortened to **telecomms**, **datacomms** or just **comms**. A computer that is on a network is said to be **networked**, **linked up**, **wired** or **online** (although *on line** can also mean switched on). A network is often called a **net**. A computer that is not on a network is often called a **standalone computer**.

LANs and WANs (see right) are the most common kinds of network. They are often linked to each other to make up more complicated networks. The *Internet**, for example, is a worldwide network made up of thousands of networks, including LANs and WANs, joined together.

(????) Passwords

Some networked computers (and some standalone computers - see above) have **password protection**. You have to type in a **password** - a secret word - before you are allowed to see the data. This stops people using the network to find, or **access**, secret data that is held on other computers. However, some people, called *hackers**, still manage to use networks to access secret data.

LANs

A **Local Area Network**, or **LAN**, links computers in the same room or building. Any piece of *hardware** linked to the LAN is called a **node**. Nodes can include *printers**, *scanners** and other *peripherals**, as well as the computers themselves. There are several kinds of LAN, including **token ring LANs**, **star LANs**, **bus LANs**, **snowflake LANs**, **optical LANs** and **ethernet LANs**. They have various kinds of layout, or **topology**.

Diagram of a token ring LAN

Computer A

Computer B

Message

Token carrying message from computer A to computer D.

Loop

Transceiver

Printer

Computer C

Computer D

In a token ring LAN, the nodes are linked to a ring, or **loop**, of *cable**. Each node has a device called a **transceiver**, which sends and receives messages. An electronic signal, called a **token**, passes continuously around the loop, picking up and delivering messages. Each message contains an electronic code called an **address**, to make sure it is dropped off when it reaches the right node.

WANs

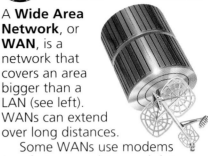

Satellite

A **Wide Area Network**, or **WAN**, is a network that covers an area bigger than a LAN (see left). WANs can extend over long distances.

Some WANs use modems (see facing page) to send data over telephone wires. Messages can also be sent in the form of radio signals. These are beamed up to **communications satellites** in space, and sent back down to their destination.

Network cables

Network systems use various kinds of *cable**. **Coaxial cable**, often used for LANs, is made up of two strands inside a wrapping called a **shield**. It can be **thick** (or **thicknet**), which is for carrying data a long way, or **thin** (also called **thinnet** or **cheapernet**) for short distances. Signals from one cable can *interfere** with another cable, damaging, or **corrupting**, the message. This interference is known as **crosstalk**.

WANs usually use existing telephone wires, which are being replaced by **fibre optic cables**. These are made of **optical fibres** which use light instead of electricity to carry data.

Fibre optic cable

Cable, 17; Computerized, 4; Graphics, 30; Hacker, 38; Hardware, 4; Interference, 17; Internet, 42; On line, 4; Peripherals, 16; Printer, 10; Scanner, 16; Sound, 32; Text, 5

Modems

A **modem** (short for **MOdulate/DEModulate**) allows computer data to be sent down a telephone line. Computers send data in the form of a series of pulses, known as **digital signals**. A modem converts, or **modulates**, these into **analog signals** (signals in the form of waves). At the other end, another modem has to **demodulate** (decode) the data back into digital signals so another computer can receive it.

How modems work

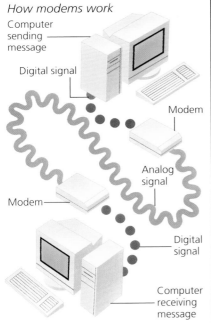

Computer sending message

Digital signal

Modem

Analog signal

Modem

Digital signal

Computer receiving message

Duplex transmission means a modem can carry data in two directions - both to and from your computer. A **full-duplex modem** can transmit in both directions at once. A **half-duplex modem** can only transmit in one direction at once. A **fax/modem** allows data to be sent to a **facsimile** or **fax machine**, which prints it out on paper.

Modems come in various shapes and sizes. A **desktop** modem is a box about 15cm (6in) long, with a *cable** which plugs into a computer. A **portable modem** is much smaller and can be used with a *notebook** computer. These are both **external modems**. A **modem card**, or **internal modem**, is a kind of *expansion card** that fits inside the *processing unit**. To use any modem, you also need a **modem interface** or **modem adaptor**. This is a type of interface that translates signals between a modem and a computer.

Desktop modem

Modem card

The speed of a modem is measured in *bits** **per second** (**bps**). A fast modem sends data at about 30,000 bits per second. Some people call bps **baud rate**. In fact, baud rate is slightly different. It is a measurement of the number of waves per second in the analog signal (see left). Some modems *compress** data (arrange it so that it uses up less bits) to make transmission faster.

A modem must be connected to a telephone line. A **dial-up modem** is used with an ordinary telephone line. A modem can be used with a special **leased line** instead, to keep it separate from the telephone line.

BABT-approved modems have been checked by the **British Approvals Board for Telecommunications**. A modem that is not BABT-approved is known as a **grey modem**.

Network words

- **Communication channel** A wire, *cable** or any kind of pathway that carries a message.
- **Bandwidth** The data-carrying capacity of a cable or any other communication channel, measured in bps (see left). A channel that can carry a lot of data has a **high bandwidth**.
- **Protocol** A system computers use to recognize each other and check data has been received. Also called **electronic etiquette** or **handshaking**.
- **Server** A computer that serves other computers on a network. A **file server** stores and organizes data that all the computers can use. A **net server** or **local server** links individual computers or small networks to big networks.
- **Mail** Messages sent to a computer over a network. (See *email** and *Internet**.)
- **Packet-switching** A way of splitting large amounts of data into small sections, or **packets**, which can be sent across a network more easily. A **PAD (Packet Assembler and Disassembler)** *program** splits up the data and puts it together again at its destination.
- **Workgroup** A group of people, usually in an office, who work together using a computer network to share and swap data.
- **Bulletin Board System (BBS)** A networked computer which network users can access and leave messages on for other users to read. You can also **download**, or copy, *files**, such as programs and *graphics**, from a BBS.
- **Host** A networked computer, especially one that provides a service, such as a BBS (see above).

*Bit, 20; Cable, 17; Compression, 23; Email, 42; Expansion card, 8; File, 25; Graphics, 30; Interface, 8; Internet, 42; Notebook, 13; Processing unit, 8; Program, 36

19

How computers work

Computers do all their calculations using a code made up of just two numbers - 0 and 1. This system is called **binary code**, or **binary**. When data is fed into a computer, it has to be converted into binary code. Information in binary code is often called **digital information**.

Bits and bytes

Each 0 or 1 is called a **bit** (short for **binary digit**). Bits usually travel around the computer in groups of eight, called **bytes**.

An example of a byte

One bit

`0 0 1 1 1 0 0 1`

The processing work in a computer is done by chips (see facing page). Electronic pathways called **buses** link the chips together, and carry data between them. Buses are used in three ways: **data buses** carry the data itself; **control buses** carry instructions telling the computer what to do with the data; and **address buses** tell the computer where in its *memory** to find or store data.

A simple bus is made up of eight *tracks**. Each track carries one bit, so the whole bus carries one byte. Bits travel in the form of electrical signals in the tracks. One kind of electrical signal represents a "1" bit. Another kind represents a "0" bit.

Diagram of a simple 8-bit bus

Bit

Track

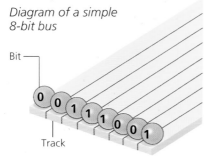

Today, most buses have more than eight tracks so they can carry more data. A **16-bit bus** has 16 tracks and carries two bytes at a time. Some computers have a **32-bit bus** or even a **64-bit bus**.

A **multiplexed bus** is a bus which can carry more than one bit on each track, using a kind of technology called **time division multiplexing**.

Buses and cards

As well as linking the chips (see facing page) in a computer, buses also contain *expansion slots**. These are slots into which you can put *expansion cards**. There are several makes and types of bus, and you can only use a particular expansion card if you have the right type of bus to put it into.

The first *IBM PC** had a 16-bit bus known as the **AT bus** or the **expansion bus**, because it was the first bus with expansion slots. This type of bus became the standard, and was soon known as the **ISA (Industry Standard Architecture) bus**. The ISA bus is not very fast, but it is still popular, because lots of expansion cards are made to fit it.

Newer kinds of bus have been developed which work much faster, such as the **MCA (Micro Channel Architecture) bus** and the **EISA (Extended ISA) bus**. These are both 32-bit buses. The EISA bus is more popular, as it is **backwardly compatible** - it can hold the older ISA cards as well as its own EISA cards.

A **local bus** is a different, faster bus system that links the *CPU** chip to the *RAM** chips. Since the *386** computer appeared, *PCs** have had both types of bus - a main bus (either

ISA, EISA or MCA) and a local bus. Expansion cards can be fitted into both types.
A diagram of the two-bus system

Key: Main bus   Local bus

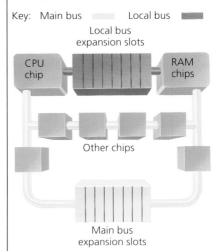

Local bus expansion slots

CPU chip

RAM chips

Other chips

Main bus expansion slots

The local bus can only hold special **local bus expansion cards**. There are two main types of local bus, each with its own type of card. The **VESA (Video Electronics Standard Association) local bus**, also called the **VL-bus**, is the usual type, and most local bus expansion cards are made to fit it. There is also a faster, but more expensive, type of local bus called the **PCI (Peripheral Component Interconnect) local bus**.

*Notebook** PCs often have **PCMCIA (Personal Computer Memory Cards International Association) expansion cards** which are small and light, like credit cards. The notebook's VESA or PCI bus is specially adapted to hold these.

PCMCIA card

*386 computer, 12; CPU, 9; Expansion card, 8; Expansion slot, 8; IBM PC, 12; Memory, 22; Notebook, 13;
PC, 4, 12; RAM, 22; Track, 8

Chips

Chips (also called **microchips**, **silicon chips** and **Integrated Circuits** or **ICs**) do the processing work inside a computer. Each chip does a particular job, such as storing or organizing data. The main chip in a computer is the *CPU**, which does calculations on data.

A chip is made of a tiny slice, or **wafer**, of a substance called **silicon**. The wafer is covered with thousands of electronic pathways, arranged in layouts called *circuits**.

Each chip is protected by a plastic case, or **housing**, with wires called **feet** connecting the chip to the computer.

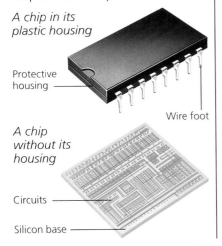

A chip in its plastic housing

Protective housing

Wire foot

A chip without its housing

Circuits

Silicon base

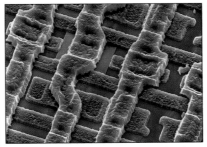

Part of a chip's surface, hundreds of times bigger than in real life.

The *architecture** of a CPU chip is very important. A **CISC** (**Complex Instruction Set Computer**) **CPU** has complicated architecture and can follow many different kinds of instructions. A **RISC** (**Reduced Instruction Set Computer**) **CPU** has simpler architecture. It follows fewer instructions, but runs faster than a CISC CPU.

 ## How chips work

Silicon, which forms the base of a chip, is a **semiconductor** - it can carry some electricity. The *circuits** covering the silicon base are made of different kinds of semiconductor. When a chip is built, the different semi-conductors are made to cross each other in certain ways, to form tiny devices called **transistors**. Bits (see facing page) pass through these transistors and are changed from 1s into 0s, or vice versa. This is how processing happens.

The transistors are arranged in patterns, or **configurations**, so that they can perform different *functions**, such as adding or comparing numbers. A simple arrangement of transistors is called a **logic gate**. There are several types. The commonest is a **nand gate**. The other types include **nor gates**, **and gates**, **or gates** and **not gates**. Arrangements of logic gates make up **flip-flops**, such as **JK-type flip-flops** and **D-type flip-flops**.

Flip-flops and logic gates are very complicated and much too small to see in real life, but they can be represented using diagrams called **logic symbols**.

A logic symbol diagram of a logic gate

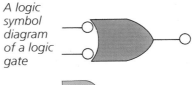

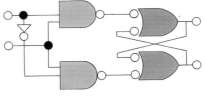

A logic symbol diagram of a D-type flip-flop

(***?) Computer words

- **Word** A group of bytes travelling on the same bus.
- **Floating point arithmetic** A way of processing very large or small numbers. The computer converts these numbers into formulae, such as as "23e-80", which are easier for it to store and work on. Normal computer arithmetic is called **fixed point arithmetic**.

- **MIPS (Millions of Instructions Per Second)** A measure of simple **processing speed** (the speed at which a computer can do calculations).
- **FLOPS (FLoating point Operations Per Second)** A measure of processing speed when **floating point operations** (calculations done using floating point arithmetic) are being used. A million FLOPS is called a **megaflop**, and a billion FLOPS is

called a **gigaflop**. These units are used to measure fast, complicated mathematical calculations on big computers.
- **Maths co-processor** An extra *CPU** chip, built into some computers, and used for mathematical calculations.
- **Clock doubling** A kind of technology that makes the CPU run twice as fast as the computer's *clock**. This makes the computer run faster.

---

*Architecture, 4; Circuit, 8; Clock, 9; CPU, 9; Function, 4

Memory and storage

Memory, which is made up of *chips**, and **storage devices**, such as disks (see facing page), hold data (information) that computers use. The main difference between them is that memory mostly holds data you are using when your computer is switched on, and storage devices hold data you need to keep when you switch your computer off. This data includes *software** and *files**.

When you want to use a piece of software or open a file, you transfer it from a storage device into the memory. This is called **loading**. Transferring data from the memory back onto a storage device is called **saving**.

This diagram shows how memory and storage devices are used.

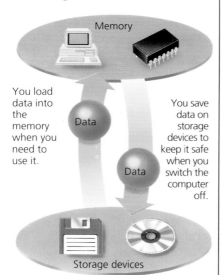

Memory

You load data into the memory when you need to use it.

Data

You save data on storage devices to keep it safe when you switch the computer off.

Data

Storage devices

The amount of data a memory chip or storage device can hold is called its **capacity**. Capacity is measured in *bytes**. A **kilobyte, Kbyte, KB** or **K** is 1024 bytes. A **megabyte**, also called a **Mbyte, MB** or **meg**, is 1024 kilobytes (about a million bytes). A **gigabyte, Gbyte, GB** or **gig** is 1024 megabytes.

RAM

RAM (Random-Access Memory) is the largest part of your computer's memory. It holds the data which you load into your computer when you want to use it (see left). RAM is **volatile** - when you switch the computer off, the data in RAM disappears. RAM is called "Random-Access Memory" because it takes the computer the same amount of time (called the **access time**) to find, or **access**, any part of a RAM *chip**. An average *PC** has about four megabytes (see left) of RAM.

The most common type of RAM, called **Dynamic RAM** or **DRAM**, holds data in the form of electrical energy. A DRAM chip contains thousands of tiny electronic devices called **capacitors** or **buckets**. Each bucket can store one *bit** (either a 1 or a 0 - the smallest unit of data a computer can hold). A capacitor can either be empty (an **empty bucket**), representing a 0, or filled up with electricity (a **full bucket**), representing a 1.

A group, or **array**, of eight buckets is called a **cell** or a **memory location**. Each cell has an **address** which the computer uses to find the data.

Static RAM is another kind of RAM. It has a faster access time than DRAM, but also costs more.

In most computers, there is also a small amount of **CMOS (Complementary Metal Oxide Semiconductor) RAM**, which keeps information such as the time and the date. It has a **RAM battery** which **refreshes** the RAM (keeps it going) while the computer is switched off, so it does not lose its data.

The most frequently used data from RAM is kept in the **cache memory**, or **cache**. This is an extra-fast RAM chip in between the main RAM chips and the *CPU**. The CPU can find data from the cache much faster than from main RAM.

Extra RAM

You can enlarge or **expand** your RAM with extra RAM *chips**, which are arranged in rows called **SIMMs (Single In-line Memory Modules)**. You can also buy *expansion cards** which contain extra RAM. Another way to expand RAM is to use **shadow RAM** or **virtual RAM**. This breaks the data into pieces called **segments** and **pages**, and stores some of them on your hard disk (see facing page) to make more space in RAM. Using shadow RAM can make a computer work slowly.

ROM

ROM stands for **Read-Only Memory**. It holds the basic instructions a computer needs to start working when you switch it on, and to control the way it works. Unlike RAM, ROM is **non-volatile** - it never loses its data. The data is held in the arrangements of the wires in ROM *chips**, and cannot be changed. ROM is called Read-Only Memory because you can only "read" it, not change, or "rewrite" it. However, some computers have a bit of **Erasable Programmable ROM**, or **EPROM**, which you can change and update.

Firmware is a kind of ROM which contains *software**. Sometimes the *operating system** is held on firmware in your computer when you buy it.

*Bit, 20; Byte, 20; Chip, 21; CPU, 9; Expansion card, 8; File, 25; Operating system, 24; PC, 4, 12; Software, 4, 24

Storage devices

Storage devices, such as disks and tapes, hold data and keep it safe while it is not being used. This is sometimes called **secondary storage**. **Internal storage devices** are inside your computer's *processing unit**, and **external storage devices** are separate from the computer. A device called a **drive** is used to **read from** (collect data from) a disk or tape, or **write to** it (add new data).

 ## Floppy disks

Floppy disks, also called **magnetic disks** or **floppies**, are external storage devices, made of flexible (but not really floppy) plastic. Data is stored as arrangements of tiny magnetic particles on the disk's surface.

Floppy disks come in various sizes, such as **3.5 inch, 5.25 inch** and **8 inch**. 3.5 inch floppy disks, also called **microfloppies, minifloppies** or **diskettes**, are the most common, and have a capacity (see facing page) of up to 2.88 megabytes of data. Floppy disks can be used to keep **back-ups** (spare copies) of your data and also for carrying data to a different computer.

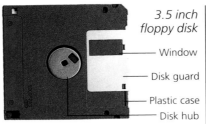

3.5 inch floppy disk

— Window
— Disk guard
— Plastic case
— Disk hub

A floppy disk fits into a computer's **floppy disk drive**. The drive spins the disk while a **read/write head** reads its data, or writes new data onto it.

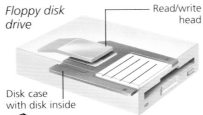

Floppy disk drive

Read/write head

Disk case with disk inside

 ## The hard disk

The **hard disk** is an internal storage device which stays permanently inside a **hard disk drive** in a computer. Hard disks work in the same way as floppies, but they are made of metal and can hold much more data. (A hard disk in a *PC** usually holds up to about 500 megabytes.) Most people use their hard disk to keep all their *software** and *files** organized in a convenient way.

(***?) ## Storage words

- **Data compression** Using a special *program** to rewrite data so that it takes up less space.
- **Tape cartridge** or **data cartridge** A storage device which holds data on magnetic tape. It uses a drive called a **tape drive, deck** or **transport**.
- **SCSI (Small Computer Systems Interface)** A kind of *interface** which can transmit data very fast. It is often used to connect disk drives (see left) to *PCs**. A **SCSI drive** (usually pronounced "scuzzy drive") is a drive which uses a SCSI.
- **Disk cache** A device which stores the most frequently used data from the hard disk, so that the computer can find it quickly.
- **Density** The amount of data a storage device can hold on a given area of its surface. For example, **high density 3.5 inch disks** have more capacity (see facing page) than **double density** ones, even though they are the same size.
- **Formatting** The surface of a disk is **formatted**, or prepared for use, by being divided into areas called **tracks** and **sectors**. The computer uses these to find the right part of a disk quickly.

 ## Optical discs

Optical discs (always spelt disc, not disk) are a kind of storage device with a very high capacity (see facing page). **Compact discs** or **CDs** are the most common kind. A CD can hold 680 megabytes of data - over 200 times more than a floppy (see above). Most CDs used in computers are *CD-ROMs**, which the user can read from, but not write to (see above). They are often used for *multimedia* software**. **WORM (Write Once Read Many) discs** can be written onto once by the user, but can be read lots of times. **Erasable optical discs**, also called **magneto-optical** or **floptical discs**, can be written onto many times.

An optical disc usually stores data as a pattern of holes, called **pits**, and flat areas, called **lands**, on its surface. It is read by an **optical disc drive**, which shines a *laser beam** at the disc. The laser light is reflected off the lands and the pits in different ways. The drive reads the data by collecting the patterns of reflected light.

Close-up of part of a CD-ROM

Land ⌐
Pit ⌐

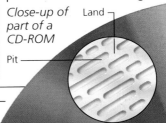

*CD-ROM, 35; File, 25; Interface, 8; Laser beam, 11; Multimedia, 35; PC, 4, 12; Processing unit, 8; Program, 36; Software, 4, 24

Software

In order to do anything useful, a computer needs instructions. These instructions are called **software**, and there are many diferent kinds.

Software is usually kept on *storage devices**, such as *disks**, when it is not being used, and loaded into a computer's *RAM** when it is needed. Software is always written in the form of *programs** (sets of instructions for doing particular things).

A computer is nearly always using, or **running**, several programs at once, on different levels. Most computers use three software levels.

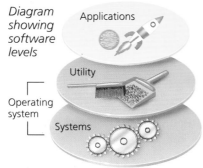

Diagram showing software levels

Applications

Utility

Operating system

Systems

Systems software runs a computer's basic *functions**, such as controlling which programs are running at any one time. **Utility software** helps you organize your data. This is known as **housekeeping**. It also includes programs called **drivers** which control, or **drive**, devices that are linked to the computer, such as the *printer**. **Applications software** programs, also called **applications**, let you do specific jobs such as writing, drawing or doing calculations.

Systems and utility software together make up the operating system (see right). This is usually already in a computer when you buy it. Applications software is usually bought separately.

The OS

An **Operating System**, or **OS**, is a set of *programs** that control and organize everything the computer does, and provide a "background" for any other software that is being used. The operating system runs all the time, while other software runs "within" it or "on top of" it. The operating system includes the user interface (see below).

Most *PCs** use an operating system called **MS-DOS** (or just **DOS**), short for **Microsoft Disk Operating System** (because it was originally just used to run *disk drives**). Other operating systems include **OS/2**, an operating system specially designed to do *multitasking**, and **UNIX**, a powerful operating system used on *workstations**. *Macs** have their own operating system, called **System 6**, **System 7**, **System 7.5** or **Mac OS**.

Some operating systems work with another similar set of programs running on top of them. For example, DOS is often used with Microsoft *Windows**.

User interfaces

The **User Interface** or **UI** is a part of the operating system (see above). It lets you communicate with, or hold a **dialogue** with, your computer. It usually consists of screens which let you choose from a range of options. A **dialogue box** is a box which appears on the screen containing a particular choice or question about what you want to do.

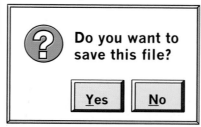

Do you want to save this file?

Yes   No

A dialogue box which helps you save* data.

• A **menu-driven user interface** shows a list, or **menu**, of options, across the top of the screen, in a panel called a **menu bar**. When you choose one, another menu called a **pull-down menu** drops below the bar, offering you a further list of options to choose from.

• A **GUI** (**Graphical User Interface**) uses little pictures called **icons** to represent some of the options it offers you. You select the icon you want using the *mouse** or *keyboard**. GUIs are easy to use and are sometimes called **WIMP** (*Windows**, **Icons, Mouse** and *Pointer**) **interfaces**. Most GUIs also use *text** and menus to ask you questions and explain things.

These icons are from Intellipoint®, a program* that lets you control the way your mouse works.

• With a **3-D user interface**, you can use your mouse to move, or **navigate**, around a 3-D world in computer space, or **digital space**. For example, the screen might show a 3-D view of a street and buildings. If you wanted to send an *email** message, you would choose the post office. This kind of user interface is sometimes called a **desktop metaphor** - a computer imitation of the real world.

Disk (drive), 23; Email, 42; Function, 4; Keyboard, 6; Mac, 12; Mouse, 7; Multitasking, 14; PC, 4, 12; Pointer, 7; Printer, 10; Program, 36; RAM, 22; Saving, 22; Storage device, 23; Text, 5; Workstation, 15; Windows, 26

Files

When you use software, you often create pieces of data, which you want to keep. A piece of data like this is called a **file**. A **data file** contains data such as *text**, numbers or *graphics**. A data file containing mainly text is called a **text file** or **document**. A **program file** (also called an **executable**) holds a *program** which is used to work on data.

When you make a file, you give it a name, or **filename**. For example, in DOS (see facing page), filenames have two parts, separated by a dot. The **identifier** (before the dot) describes the data in the file. The **file extension** (after the dot) shows what kind of file it is.

Parts of a DOS filename

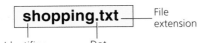

These are some of the DOS file extensions you might see:
- **.txt** A text file
- **.sys** A file containing systems software (see facing page)
- **.exe** An executable (a name for a program file). A **.com** file is another type of executable file.

Most operating systems (see facing page) have a **file manager**, a program which shows you a list of your files and helps you organize them into groups called **directories** and **sub-directories**.

Part of a file manager

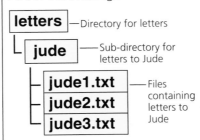

You **open** a file to start working on it, and to finish, you **close** it. You have to *save** a file before closing it, if you want to keep everything you have done. You can **move** files around in the file manager, **copy** files between your *hard disk** and *floppy disks**, and **delete** or **erase** (remove) files.

 # Packages

A piece of applications software is called a **software package**. A package containing several applications is called **integrated software** or a **software suite**. Software can be **custom-written** (written specially for your needs) or **shrinkwrapped** (mass-produced). **Bundled software** is software sold with a computer.

A software package usually comes in a box containing *floppy disks** and **documentation** (booklets), including a handbook or **manual**, which explains how to install and use the software.

A typical software package

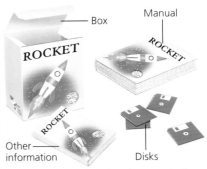

Software can also be copied, or *downloaded**, from one computer to another, if they are *networked**. You can often get **freeware** (free software) in this way. **Shareware** (also called **honourware**) is similar, but you may have to pay to use it.

 # Installing

You usually **install** applications software (see facing page), or transfer it from *floppy disks** onto your *hard disk**, so that you can find it easily. When you want to use an application, you *load** it (transfer it into *RAM**). There are many different applications for creating *graphics**, playing *games**, designing, learning, and lots of other things. You can see some of them on the following pages.

Screen showing games software

Screen showing graphics software

Computer-Aided Design (CAD*)

*CAD, 29; Downloading, 19; Floppy disk, 23; Games, 34; Graphics, 30; Hard disk, 23; Loading, 22; Network, 18, 42; Program, 36; RAM, 22; Saving, 22; Text, 5

Basic applications

Most computers come with a set of basic *applications** *software**, or **core applications**. These enable you to do everyday tasks, such as writing, doing calculations, and keeping lists of data. The computer may also come with an *operating system**, such as *DOS**.

You can only use an application if it is in the right **format** - designed to work with your operating system. For example, if you use DOS with Microsoft Windows (see below), you can only use applications that are designed specifically "**for Windows**".

Microsoft Windows

Microsoft Windows® is a well-known *operating system** which works with *PCs**. It uses rectangular areas of the screen, called **windows**, to display data. One window can take up the whole screen, or several smaller windows can be displayed at once, showing data from different *files**, and even from different *applications**. You can easily swap from one window to another. A window can be **maximized** (made as big as possible), **minimized** (made as small as possible), or **iconified** (made into a little picture, or *icon**).

Word processing

A **Word Processing** (**WP**) **program***, is a type of *software** that helps you write letters, stories and any other kind of *text**. You can change or **edit** your piece of writing, or *document**, as much as you like. Some word processing words are listed here.

• **WYSIWYG** (**What You See Is What You Get**) display, pronounced "wizziwig". This means that the document looks the same on the screen as it does when you print it out.

• **Word wrap** This means that when you get to the end of a line, the next word automatically appears on the line below.

• **Hyphenation** Putting hyphens into the text. Some WP programs do this automatically.

• **Page layout** The way text is arranged on the page. You can set **margins** (borders at the edges of the page) and **headers** and **footers** (separate pieces of text, such as page numbers, at the top and bottom of the page).

• **Tab** (short for **tabulate**) This *function** lets you preset different margins, so you can set out data in columns and rows easily.

• **Justified text** Text that lines up on both the left-hand side and the right-hand side.

• **Block** A piece of text. You can choose a block of text and **cut and paste** it (move it to another part of the document or another *file**), or **copy** it (repeat it).

• **Formatting text** Changing the appearance of the text. For example, text can be **bold**, **underlined** or *italic*.

• **Typeface** or **font** The style of the **type** (letters and numbers). There are thousands of different fonts, such as **Times**, **Helvetica**, Casablanca Antique, Kids, and VIKING.

• **Point size** or **type size** The height of the type. A **point** is $1/72$ of an inch. This sentence is written in 10.5 point text.

• **Spellcheck** This checks your spelling and suggests several replacements for any words it doesn't recognize.

• **Wordcount** This counts the words in your document.

• **Search and replace** This function lets you change a particular word (for example a name) into another word, throughout the text.

• **TWP** (**Technical Word Processor**) A word processing program made for writing technical or scientific data, such as mathematical formulae.

Screen showing word-processed text

Margin   Header   "Palatino" typeface   Selected block

Communication

Communication is the act of sending out  or signals to make known a fact, express a feeling and so on. Animals communicate for many reasons such as to attract mates, deter predators, show fear or to keep in contact with others.

Visual signals travel faster than sound, but most can only be seen over short distances. As in **humans**, an animal's *body posture* can signal <u>different moods.</u>

Page 8   **Wordcount:71**

Footer   Italic text   Underlined text   Bold text   "Gill sans" typeface   Wordcount

**Applications, 24; Document, 25; DOS, 24; File, 25; Function, 4; Icon, 24; Operating system, 24; PC, 4, 12; Program, 36; Software, 4, 24; Text, 5*

Financial software

Businesses often use **financial** or **business** *software** to do calculations on finances (money).

Using a spreadsheet (see right)

There are several different kinds of financial software:
- **Personal financial management software** This keeps records of your private spending.
- **Business accounting software** Software that helps businesses keep financial records and organize wages and tax.
- **Financial analysis software** This is used by banks and businesses to examine financial data and predict, or forecast, future profits and spending.

Most financial software *programs** use **spreadsheets** or **worksheets**. These are mathematical tables which show figures in horizontal **rows** and vertical **columns**.

Part of a spreadsheet

	Oct	Nov	Dec
Clothes	32.50	74.96	40.45
Going out	40.05	24.55	**55.40**
Bus fares	24.50	19.10	30.00
Total	97.05	118.61	125.85

Label · Cell pointer · Label · Value · Calculated cell

The title of a column or row is called a **label**. The information named by one label is called a **range** (for example, all the figures in the "Clothes" row). A single box in a spreadsheet is called a **cell**. You use the *mouse** or *keyboard** to move a **cell pointer**. This highlights one cell at a time so that you can write or change the number (called a **value**) in the cell.

A spreadsheet can also have **calculated cells**. These automatically add up the values in each row or column, and automatically change when you change the values. You can change the information in just one cell, row or column (a **local change**) or change the values for the whole spreadsheet (a **global change**).

Databases

Database or **databank** *software** is used to manage databases - stores of information. It helps you find the data you want quickly and easily. For example, a club might use a database to keep a list of all its members. A **File Processing System** (**FPS**) is software for working with simple databases. A **DataBase Management System** (**DBMS**) is more powerful and can analyze data in lots of ways.

Each type of data in a database is called a **field** - for example, names, addresses and so on. A single piece of data is called an **entry**. Some databases help you to enter details by giving you a **form**, a screen where you fill in a collection of entries, called a **record**, about one particular thing. The way the fields and records are organized is called the **data hierarchy**. Some databases are very complicated, with hundreds of fields and millions of records. A **multimedia*** **database** has **visual data** (pictures) as well as *text**.

A **search** *function** can find particular entries in a database, and a **sort function** can sort out data into different orders, such as alphabetical order. A **filter function** sorts data into groups - for example, you could use a filter to make a list of all the people in one town or city.

Databases are also used in other ways. A **videotex system**, such as Teletext, uses a database to store information such as television schedules or weather forecasts. You can see the data on your television screen, using a remote control **keypad** (a small *keyboard**) to change from one **page** (screen of data) to another.

A **medical expert system** (sometimes called a **medical jukebox**) uses a database to hold large amounts of medical information. Doctors use it to help diagnose illnesses.

A form showing data about a member of a club

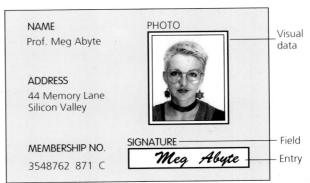

NAME
Prof. Meg Abyte

PHOTO — Visual data

ADDRESS
44 Memory Lane
Silicon Valley

MEMBERSHIP NO.
3548762 871 C

SIGNATURE — Field
Meg Abyte — Entry

Function, 4; Keyboard, 6; Mouse, 7; Multimedia, 35; Program, 36; Software, 4, 24; Text, 5

Design software

Design *software** is used for designing all sorts of things, from books, buildings and aeroplanes to transport routes, machines and maps. It provides a **computer simulation**, or imitation, of real life, allowing you to create all kinds of layouts and drawings.

*This map was created using GIS** (Geographical Information Systems), a kind of design software for making maps.*

 ## Design tools

When you use design *software**, you draw and **manipulate** (change around) your designs using a range of different *functions** called **tools**. You choose a tool by selecting an *icon** from a group of icons known as a **toolbox** or **palette**. With a **customizable toolbox** or **palette**, you can choose the tools you want and arrange them to suit your own needs.

Lines called **guides** and **rulers** can be laid out to help you position your design correctly. A fixed arrangement of guides and rulers is called a **template**. For example, if you were designing a book, you would probably use the same template for each page.

The design you are creating might be much bigger than the screen on your *monitor**. To help you see the whole design, you can **view** (look at) the design at different sizes, **zoom** (look at part of the design in close-up), and *scroll** or **pan** (move around the design to look at different parts of it).

 ## DTP

DTP (**DeskTop Publishing**) is a *computerized** way of designing the layout of *text** and pictures in publications, such as books, magazines and leaflets. DTP *software** lets you create, move and change text and pictures in all sorts of ways. You can write text onto the screen, but cannot create pictures. These have to be imported (see below).

• **Page** An imitation on the screen of an actual page. Designers often work on two facing pages (called a **spread**) at one time.

• **Text box** or **frame** A frame around a piece of text. You can move and rearrange the text by moving the text box.

• **Import** To bring other data, such as a *graphic**, from another *file** or *application** and put, or **place**, it on your page.

• **Resize** To change the size of a picture or text box. You can also **rotate** (spin), **skew** (twist), **crop** (trim) and **stretch** pictures and text boxes.

• **Text wrapping** or **wrapping** Arranging text in a shape that fits neatly around a picture.

• **Tracking** or **kerning** Changing the space between *characters**, to make them more squashed together (called **tight tracking**) or more spaced apart (called **loose tracking**).

• **Edit tool** You choose this when you want to write text onto the page or make changes to the text already there.

• **Drawing tools** These are used to draw rectangles, circles, lines (called **rules**) and ovals on the page. A **line *function*** lets you choose the thickness of the lines or outlines and a **fill function** lets you fill in shapes with colour or a pattern.

*A spread from a book being designed with a DTP program**

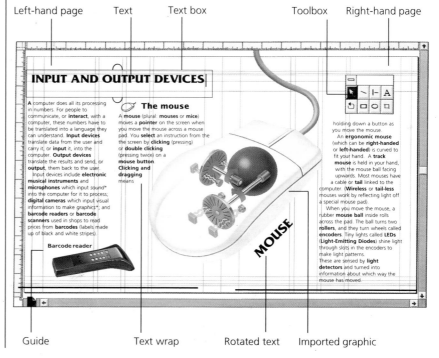

Left-hand page · Text · Text box · Toolbox · Right-hand page

Guide · Text wrap · Rotated text · Imported graphic

Applications, 24; Character, 6; Computerized, 4; File, 25; Function, 4; GIS, 48; Graphics, 30; Icon, 24; Monitor, 7; Program, 36; Scroll, 6; Software, 4, 24; Text, 5

CAD

CAD (Computer-Aided Design) *software** is used by designers to draw 3-D designs of buildings, vehicles, furniture and all sorts of other things.

The first stage is to make a **wire frame** or **wire mesh design**, which is made up of a network of thin lines.

Wire frame design for a jet plane

Then the wire frame design is **rendered**, or made solid-looking. The spaces can be filled in with colour, or with patterns called **hatching**. Some CAD software uses a technique called **ray tracing** to make the object look as if a light is shining on it from one side. The imaginary space the design is in is called the **model space**.

CAD software makes it easy to draw, or **define**, shapes using special *functions**. **Filleting** and **trimming functions** automatically make your drawing neater and more accurate. You can choose perfect circles and rectangles from a selection of pre-defined shapes called **primitives**. An **aerial view function** lets you see the whole of your design in one corner of the screen, while you look at one part in close-up.

Rendered design

Solid-looking surface

The object is made to look as if light is shining on it.

For complicated designs, a method called **hiding** can be used. Different levels, or **layers**, of an object can be built up on top of each other. One layer could show the outside of a building, while the layer beneath showed the water pipes and electricity wires inside.

CAD software design for a part of an engine

CAD software design for a building

Testing

CAT (Computer-Aided Testing) *software** is used to test CAD designs (see above). You can use it to **visualize**, or see, a design behaving like a real object. There are several types of testing including **resistance testing**, which imitates the flow of air or water around an object, and **crash testing**, which can simulate a vehicle in a crash.

One testing method is called **finite element analysis**. A design, such as a car windscreen, is divided into small pieces called **elements**, and each element is given **material properties** - descriptions of the weight and qualities of different substances, such as glass. Then you can **model**, or imitate, a real situation. For example, you could see where and how the windscreen would break in a crash.

*Virtual Reality** can be used to let testers "walk around" inside a design for a large structure, such as a museum or a railway station, before anything is built. This helps prevent possible problems such as congestion.

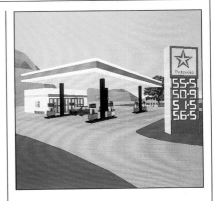

Part of a virtual reality design for a garage. You could "go into" this design and explore the garage as if it were real.

Graphics software

Graphics *software** can be used to create pictures, or to change and *process** pictures that you put into a computer. **Computer graphics** are any kind of pictures made or processed by a computer.

Computer graphics are sometimes called **Computer-Generated Imagery** (**CGI**). Processing graphics is called **image processing** or **Digital Image Processing** (**DIP**).

There are two types of graphics. Both are made up of *pixels** - tiny dots on the screen of your *monitor**. With **bitmapped graphics**, each pixel is controlled individually. With **character graphics**, often used on older computers, the pixels are controlled in groups.

Graphics software has many creative uses, such as making computer art, cartoons, and special effects for films. Graphics are also used in *games**, *CAD** and other software.

Analysis graphics are used to represent information in a visual way to make it easier to understand - for example, by turning information in the form of numbers into pictures, called **graphs** or **charts**.

A pie chart created using analysis graphics

Presentation graphics are used to make visual information more interesting, for example by making it 3-D or more colourful.

The same pie chart enhanced using presentation graphics

Hardware

You sometimes need special *hardware** to use certain kinds of graphics *software**.

A **graphics card** or **video card** is an *expansion card** which improves the quality of graphics on your computer. You often need a graphics card if you want to have good **video graphics**, or moving pictures, which need a lot of *memory** and *processing power**. Some graphics cards contain a kind of *RAM** called **VRAM** (**Video Random-Access Memory**). This helps video graphics work faster.

You might also use a *graphics tablet** or **graphics pad**. You draw on this with a special pen or **stylus**, and your drawing appears on the screen. A **pressure-sensitive stylus** lets you make thicker lines by pressing harder, like a real pen.

Digitizer mouse

A **digitizing tablet** is a very sensitive type of graphics tablet used for animation and retouching (see facing page) and *CAD** software. It is used with a very accurate *mouse** called a **digitizer mouse**.

Paint packages

A **paint package** is a piece of *software** which lets you create your own graphics. Using a graphics tablet (see above) or a *mouse**, you can draw and paint in different styles, known as **brushes**. **Roller** and **spraycan** are examples of styles. You can choose different brush widths, and more advanced paint packages have **pressure-sensitive brushes** which draw different thicknesses depending on how hard you press. You choose colours, styles and so on from a **paint palette**, a kind of *toolbox** on the screen.

Pictures created using paint packages

Some packages have **user-definable brushes** and **palettes**. This means you can design your own styles (called **customized styles**) and keep them for whenever you need them.

Paint effects

Paint effects packages let you change pictures that already exist. For example, you can *scan** a picture into the computer and then make it look like an oil painting or a drawing, or like a blurred photograph. The different effects are called **filters**.

These pictures have been processed using graphics filters.

*CAD, 29; Expansion card, 8; Games, 34; Graphics tablet, 16; Hardware, 4; Memory, 22; Monitor, 7; Mouse, 7; Pixel, 7; Processing, 4; Processing power, 9; RAM, 22; Scanning, 16; Software, 4, 24; Toolbox, 28

Computer art

Graphics *software** is used to create amazing works of **computer art**. Some are done with paint packages (see facing page), and others use mathematical formulae, such as **fractals** and **sets**, to build up complicated patterns. Graphics software is also used to create **random-dot stereograms**. These seem like abstract patterns, but if you look at them in a certain way, you can see a 3-D image.

Computer art created using a fractal formula

Compositing

Compositing or **image compositing** means putting together parts of different pictures to make them look like one new picture. You can also do this with moving pictures (**video compositing**). For example, you can composite two photographs to make it look as if two people have had their photograph taken together, even if they have never met. You can also **delete** or **edit out** (remove) parts of pictures and fill in the space with something else, or change parts of pictures to make them a different size or shape. This is called **retouching** or **touching up**.

Animation

Animation means making moving pictures. **Computer animation** means using graphics *software** to make or edit animated pictures. Animation *applications**, or **digital cartooning systems**, let you create images and make them move. **Multilayered 2-D animations** show flat characters in front of flat backgrounds. **3-D animations** show three-dimensional characters and backgrounds.

Animations are made up of a series of still pictures put together in sequence to look like moving pictures. Each still picture is called a **frame** or **cel**.

Some computer animation techniques are described here.

• **Physical modelling** Creating a **model**, or 3-D shape, on the screen to use in a 3-D animation. **Polygonal modelling** means creating the model out of shapes with straight edges. **Spline-based modelling** means making the model out of curved shapes.

• **Lofting** Putting a coloured or textured surface, or **skin**, on a model shape.

• **Data capture** or **grabbing** Filming or photographing real objects to use as models, instead of creating models on screen. **Photogrammetry** and **rotoscoping** are ways of filming an object from lots of different angles.

• **Inbetweening** To do this, the animator marks points, called **keys**, on two shapes. The computer fills in all the stages in between, so it looks as if one shape has turned into the other.

• **Flocking algorithm** A *program** that can help animate a number of objects at once, such as a crowd of people.

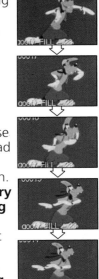

Inbetweening

Special effects

Graphics *software** is used to make many kinds of special effects for films. **Morphing** means changing one film image into another, using inbetweening (see above). **Texture mapping** means sticking a new surface, called a **mask**, onto an object. One person's face can even be stuck onto another's body. You can also distort parts of a person or object, and mix animated characters with real actors in the same film.

This animated monster was created for a science fiction film using graphics software.

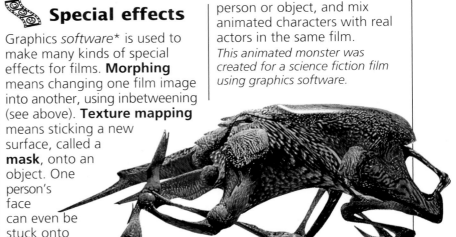

n/a

Sound and music software

Sound *software** is software for *processing** sounds. Some sound software can recognize the human voice, and imitate speech. Other software is used to mix musical sounds, or create completely new sounds. Processing sounds on a computer is called **audio processing** or **Digital Audio Processing (DAP)**. **Digital sound** or **computer-generated sound** is sound created using a computer.

Any sound that you can hear exists in the form of **sound waves** which travel through the air to your ears. These waves are a kind of *analog** signal. Computers can only work using a *digital** signal (a signal made up of *bits** instead of waves). A device called an **Analog-Digital (AD) converter** converts sound waves into digital signals so they can be processed, and a **Digital-Analog (DA) converter** turns them back into sounds.

Sound cards

If you want to use sound *software** on a *personal computer**, you usually need to add a **sound card**, a type of *expansion card**. Sound cards are usually either 8-*bit** or 16-bit. **8-bit sound cards** give less realistic sound. **16-bit sound cards** can give **CD-quality sound** (sound that is as realistic as a music *CD**). Some sound cards have a **synthesizer chip** which **synthesizes**, or imitates, real sounds. Others have a **wave table**, a store of recordings of sounds. These are called **samples**.

Mixing music

Most modern music is put together, or **mixed**, using computers. The musicians record their music, or **musical input**, into a *computer system** called a **MIDI** (**Musical Instrument Digital Interface**) **system**. The recordings are then changed or **edited**, using a control desk called a **mixing desk**. Unwanted noises can be removed using a **digital noise reduction system** or **noise gate**. The recordings can then be arranged, or **sequenced**, and joined, or **spliced**, together to make the final result.

MIDI recording *software* lets you mix music on a normal *PC**, if you have a sound card (see left). You can see the music in written form, and edit it using all the features of a mixing desk.

Screen showing MIDI recording software

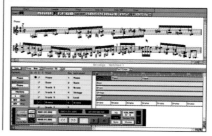

Talking

Voice recognition *software* can analyze and recognize human speech. It usually works by **word recognition** - that is, recognizing the sounds of individual words when they are spoken separately. Word recognition software converts each word into a pattern, and then compares the patterns with each other to work out which word is which. This method is called **pattern-matching**.

Word recognition software is usually used in **voice-controlled *word processors***, **dictation software** or **voice-input systems**. You speak into a microphone and your words appear written on the screen. You can use specially *programmed** **voice commands** to give other instructions, so you don't have to use your hands at all. This is ideal for people who have *RSI** or other injuries or disabilities.

Voice recognition software usually has to "learn" to recognize a particular voice before it can work properly. It does this by building up a **voice file**, a record of a person's **acoustic models** (patterns representing speech). It then compares the words it "hears" to these models.

A woman using DragonDictate voice recognition software.

Speech synthesis software is software that imitates human speech. One type, called a **text-to-voice system**, can turn written words into spoken words which the user can hear. This is useful for blind people and for people who can write, but can't speak very clearly.

The screen in this picture shows the pattern made by the word "baby".

32 *Analog, 19; Bit, 20; CD, 23; Chip, 21; Computer system, 4; Digital, 4, 19; Expansion card, 8; Personal computer (PC), 4, 12; Processing, 4; Program(ming), 36; RSI, 39; Software, 4, 24; Word processing, 26*

♪♫♪ Instruments

Electronic or **digital musical instruments**, such as **electronic keyboards** and **electronic pianos**, are *computerized** instruments. They store digital sound (see facing page) in the form of *digital** code. This is converted into sounds you can hear by a Digital-Analog converter (see facing page) in the instrument.

Some computerized instruments, like the **electronic drum kit** in the picture, are played normally. Others, such as a **drum machine** or a **synthesizer** (a machine which imitates real sounds) can be *programmed** to create different digital sounds and play them in different sequences.

Electronic music synthesiser

Liquid Crystal Display

Volume control

YAMAHA W7

These controls let you "bend" or distort sounds.

These buttons let you create different kinds of sound.

Keyboard

Control unit

Drum pad

Stand

Foot pedal for bass drum

Electronic drum kit

Electronic musical instruments are usually **MIDI-compatible**. This means they have a **MIDI socket**, a socket which allows them to be plugged into a MIDI system (see facing page).

♪♫♪ Music styles

Several different styles of music are made using sound *software**. **Ambient music** is gentle, atmospheric music, often made by mixing samples (see facing page) of sounds from nature. It often has special computer *graphics** called **visuals** to go with it. **Techno** is fast dance music, often completely computer-generated using a synthesizer (see above).

Electro-acoustic music is serious electronic music (not pop) that brings together computer and traditional music. In France, a centre called **IRCAM** (**Institut de Recherche et de Coordination Acoustique/ Musique**) explores ways in which computers can create musical sounds, especially for live or **real-time performances**. Pierre Boulez is a famous electro-acoustic composer.

Sound software is also used to make weird music and **sound effects** (special or unusual sounds) for *games** and films. This is done using sound software *programs** called **effects algorithms**.

Ambient music graphics, or "visuals"

♪♫♪ Music storage

Music takes up a lot of storage space in a *computer system**, and does not always fit on *floppy disks**. It can be stored on *optical discs** or on **Digital Audio Tape** (**DAT**), a kind of cassette tape.

Music that is sold in the shops can be stored in a *digital** form on *compact discs** or on a kind of tape called a **Digital Compact Cassette** (**DCC**).

Digital Compact Cassette player

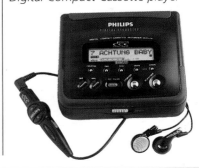

*Compact disc, 23; Computerized, 4; Computer system, 4; Digital, 4, 19; Floppy disk, 23; Games, 34; Graphics, 30; Optical disc, 23; Program(ming), 36; Software, 4, 24

33

Games, entertainment and education

Computers can be used for fun, and for learning and training. **Computer games software*** is one of the most popular of all types of software. Some games, especially those for children, are designed to be educational as well. Multimedia software (see facing page) is often both entertaining and educational, and is sometimes called **infotainment** or **edutainment software**.

 **Games**

There are many different types of computer games, also called **video games**. You can play an **arcade game**, a large, *dedicated** game-playing machine, in an amusement arcade, or a tiny **hand-held** or **pocket computer game** which can be carried anywhere. **Games computers** or **games consoles** are games machines which you plug into a television. You can also play a wide range of games on a *personal computer**.

A hand-held computer game

People who play computer games are called **gamers**. A computer game's action, or **gameplay**, is represented by *graphics** and *sound**. **Video-quality graphics** are high-quality graphics that look like film. With **real-time graphics**, the action is realistic and runs at the same speed as real life. A **sprite** is an animated character on the screen. Games are usually played using a *joystick**.

Here are some of the many types of games *software**.
- **Combat**, **hack'n'slash** or **action game** A fighting game.

Screen showing a combat game

- **Adventure game** A game in which you explore a territory, such as a castle, jungle or alien planet. **Role-playing** and **fantasy games** are similar.

- **Space combat** or **space war games** Fighting games involving battles in space.

- **Simulation games** These recreate the experience of flying a plane (**flight simulation**), or driving a vehicle. In **racing games**, you race against other vehicles or planes.
- **Topographical games** These let you control an imaginary city or civilization, using various methods of government.
- **Strategy games** Strategy games let you play one side in a battle or conflict. You are given plenty of time to plan your moves carefully.
- **Sports games** There are lots of these, such as computer golf, soccer and baseball.

 Virtual Reality

Virtual Reality (**VR**) means using 3-D *graphics** to create an imaginary world, or **virtual world**, which surrounds the user. You can use VR to play games or explore imaginary places.

You need special **VR gear** (equipment) to use VR. A **VR headset** or **head-mounted display** shows graphics on a screen in front of your eyes. As you turn your head, the picture on the screen moves around too, so it feels as if you are in a 3-D world. A **dataglove** or **VR glove** is a glove with **pressure pads** which make your hand feel as if it is picking up objects or touching surfaces. You use a kind of *mouse**, called a **VR mouse**, **3-D mouse** or **virtual mouse**, to move around in **virtual space** - the imaginary space you are exploring.

A Virtual Reality user wearing VR gear

Screen in front of eyes, showing 3-D picture

Headset

Dataglove

3-D mouse

Cables

*Dedicated computer, 15; Graphics, 30; Joystick, 16; Mouse, 7; Personal computer, 4, 12; Software, 4, 24; Sound, 32

Multimedia

Multimedia means using computers to combine *text**, *sound**, *graphics** and video. **Multimedia *software*** usually comes on a **CD-ROM (Compact Disc-Read-Only Memory)**, a kind of *compact disc**.

Multimedia software includes games, information CD-ROMs (or "**electronic books**"), and other types of educational software. Most CD-ROMs are **interactive** - you take part in what happens and choose the things you want to see and hear, using a *mouse**. For example, in a multimedia CD-ROM about nature, you might look up the word "parrot" and choose from a photograph of a parrot, a **digital video clip** (a short piece of moving film), a sound recording of a parrot squawking, some text to read, and a map showing where parrots live.

To use multimedia, you need a set of extra *hardware** called a **multimedia bundle** or **kit**. This includes a **CD-ROM *drive*** for playing CD-ROMs, **speakers** or **headphones** so you can hear the sounds, and a *sound card** and a *graphics card**. Some computers, called **MPCs**

A Multimedia Personal Computer or MPC

Microphone lets you record your own sounds.

Left speaker

Screen

Right speaker (two speakers give realistic sound effects)

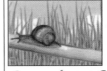

Headphones let you listen to sounds.

CD-ROM drive for playing CD-ROMs

Joystick

(**Multimedia Personal Computers**) are sold **multimedia-ready** or **multimedia-prepared** - ready fitted with multimedia equipment.

Some multimedia software uses a system called **hypertext**. In hypertext, some words, called **hypertext words**, are highlighted. If you *click** on a hypertext word, the screen shows more information about that subject. **Hypermedia** is similar, but works with pictures as well as text.

Screens from a CD-ROM on nature

 # Learning

Computer *software** can help people learn in all sorts of ways. Educational CD-ROMs (see above) invite the user to select answers or objects from a choice on the screen, using the *mouse**. This is called **interactive learning**, **collaborative learning**, or "**point-and-click" learning**. Multimedia software (see

above) is also useful for learning subjects that involve *sound**, such as music and languages.

Simulation training means using computer *graphics** or Virtual Reality (see facing page) to train pilots, doctors and other workers. The computer simulates (imitates) the situation they will have to work in, so they can practise and make mistakes without causing any harm.

This machine for training pilots simulates an aeroplane's cockpit.

*Clicking, 7; Compact disc, 23; Drive, 23; Graphics, 30; Graphics card, 30; Hardware, 4; Mouse, 7; Software, 4, 24; Sound, 32; Sound card, 32; Text, 5

Programming

A computer program is a set of instructions which a computer uses to do a particular task. Computer programs are pieces of *software**. Writing computer programs is called **programming**. Although computers seem very clever, a computer can't do anything unless somebody writes a program to tell it how. Computer programs are written in programming languages (see right). The words and symbols used to write a program are called **code**. The way a program solves problems is called **program logic**.

Program makers

Most programs are written by specially trained **computer programmers**. Many of these work for **software houses** or **software publishers**, companies that produce *software packages**. Others work for companies called **computer consultancies**, which write software to order, according to their customers' own requirements. As well as programmers, companies like these have **software engineers** and **software designers** who decide what kind of software is needed and how it will work.

Large companies often have an **applications development department** which produces software just for their company. They have *systems analysts** to find out what software is needed, and programmers to write it.

Creating new software is called **software development**. Some programmers, such as *applications** **programmers** and *systems** **programmers**, specialize in writing certain types of software.

Languages

Computers use a language called *binary code** or **machine code**. Writing programs in machine code is very difficult and slow, so a **programming language** is used to write the program in a code called the **source code** or the **source program**. Other programs then translate this into machine code.

High-level programming languages are made up of words, just like real languages, and are the easier type to use. They are translated by either an interpreter program or a compiler program. An **interpreter program** translates the source code line by line as the program is *running**. A **compiler program** translates the whole program into chunks of a simpler code, called the **object code**. A program called a **linker** then links the chunks together to make an *executable** - a program the computer can run.

Low-level programming languages are made up of numbers and symbols. They are translated by programs called **assemblers**.

Programming language levels

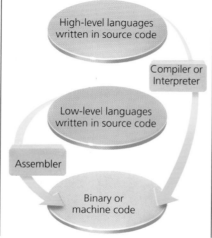

High-level languages written in source code

Compiler or Interpreter

Low-level languages written in source code

Assembler

Binary or machine code

Several programming languages are listed below. They are all high-level languages. Some are **problem-oriented languages** - languages designed for a particular purpose.

- **BASIC (Beginner's All-purpose Symbolic Instruction Code)** An easy language which is used to teach programming.
- **Logo** This simple language was invented by a scientist called Professor Seymour Papert, to help children learn about programming. Logo instructions control the movements of a *computerized** *robot** turtle, which draws pictures by moving around the floor holding a pen.

Seymour Papert's turtle

Picture

- **FORTRAN (FORmula TRANslation)** A language often used to write mathematical and scientific *software**.
- **COBOL (COmmon Business Oriented Language)** Made for writing business programs, such as payroll (wages) software.
- **Pascal** A language used by computer scientists, and often taught to computer students.
- **C** and **C++** Advanced languages, widely used for general programming.
- **Ada** An advanced language designed for military uses.
- **PROLOG (PROgramming in LOGic)** A very advanced language used mainly for *artificial intelligence** software.
- **4GL (Fourth Generation Language)** A name for programming languages that resemble human language.

Applications, 24; Artificial intelligence, 45; Binary code, 20; Computerized, 4; Executable, 25; Robot, 15; Running, 24; Software, 4, 24; Software package, 25; Systems (software), 24; Systems analyst, 14

Writing programs

There are usually three main stages in writing a program: designing, coding and testing.

Designing the program involves deciding what the program should do and how it should work. The programmer draws a diagram called a **flowchart** showing the different stages of the program. (A **macro flowchart** is rougher and more general.) The program may then be written out in **pseudocode**, or normal words.

Next, the programmer writes, or **codes**, the program in source code (see facing page), using **software tools** - programs which help write code. These include an **editor** or **text editor** (a kind of *word processing** program) and a **debug tool** or **debugger**, which helps find **bugs**, or mistakes. There are lots of ways to code one program. Coding a program well is called elegant **programming**.

When the program is written, the programmer *runs** it to see if it works. This is called **alpha testing**. The program is also tested by a sample of users called **beta testers**. Any bugs are corrected, and the programmer makes **tweaks** (small changes). This is called **debugging** or **bug fixing**.

Maintenance

Even when a program has been published (sold to the public), it can still have bugs (see left). **Program maintenance** means checking and improving a piece of *software** throughout its **life cycle** (the period of time when it is in public use). The programmer writes a detailed description of how the program works, called **program documentation**. This helps other programmers to **reprogram** or **reconfigure** (rewrite) parts of the code. The company that produced the software usually also has a **user support service**. Users can telephone or *email** the service if they need help, and can report any bugs they find.

When a program has been improved, it is often released as a new **version**. Many programs go through dozens of different versions during their life cycles.

Software versions

Program words

• **Program decomposition** Splitting a programming job into sections called **modules** or **segments**, which can be written by different programmers.
• **Algorithm** or **routine** A piece of code which does a particular job. Programmers keep a selection of algorithms, called an **algorithm library** or **program library**, to use instead of writing new code.
• **SQA** (**Software Quality Assurance**) Making sure a program is ready to be published, using **software metrics** - methods of measuring how well a program works and giving it a score.
• **SLOC** (**Source Lines Of Code**) The number of lines of source code (see facing page) a programmer writes per day or month. Used to measure a programmer's speed.
• **Loop** Part of a program that is repeated several times.
• **Nest** A piece of code inside another piece of the same type, such as a loop within a loop.
• **Top-down programming** A name for the most common method, or **approach**, for writing programs.

A flowchart, pseudocode and source code for a simple password* program.

Flowchart

```
Start
  ↓
Print message
  ↓
Get user input ←──── Print "Error"
  ↓                        ↑
Check password ────────────┘
  ↓         If password is wrong
If password is right
  ↓
Print "OK"
  ↓
End
```

Pseudocode

```
WHILE password
not OK

    PRINT "Enter
    today's password"

    GET input from
    user

    IF password OK
    PRINT "OK"

    ELSE PRINT "Error"
    END IF

END
```

Source code (the program)
written in C (see facing page)

```c
#define PASSWORD "robot"

main ( )  {
  int password_ok = 0;
  char input [80] ;

    while (!password _ok)  {

      printf ("\nEnter today's
      password:  \n)" ;

      gets (input) ;

      if (strcmp (input,
      PASSWORD) == 0)  {
        printf ("Password
        accepted. \n") ;
        password_ok = 1;
      }
      else printf ("%s is not
      today's password!\n",
      input) ;
    }
}
```

Computer problems and solutions

Computer systems* are complicated and can go wrong. For example, hardware* can be faulty and software* can have bugs*. Computers are also at risk from crime, such as hacking, virus-writing and pirating. Using computers could even damage your health.

Systems failure

Computer failure is often called **systems failure** or **crashing**. A computer that is not working is said to be **down** or **crashed**. A **hang-up** means your computer does not respond when you try to use the mouse* or keyboard*. The amount of time that a computer system* is not working is known as the **equipment downtime**.

When computers fail, you can often lose the data you are working on. This is why you need to back up* (keep copies of) all your data. Many types of software* have functions* such as **autobackup** and **autosave**, which automatically keep copies of your data as you work.

Here are some different kinds of computer problems and some possible solutions.

• **Static interference** Damage caused to data by static electricity (a form of electricity which builds up in objects). An **anti-static** or **earthed mouse mat** can help to stop this.

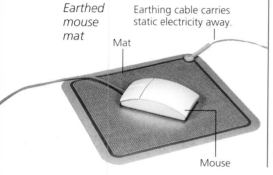

Earthed mouse mat
Earthing cable carries static electricity away.
Mat
Mouse

• **Screen burn** or **burn-in** happens when you leave the same image on your screen for a long time and it becomes permanently imprinted on the screen glass. To avoid this, you can use a program* called a **screen saver**. This replaces the image with a moving picture after a certain amount of time.

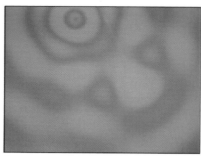

A screen saver program

• **Buggy chip** A chip* that has something wrong with it. The problem can sometimes be cured using a program called a **software patch** to replace the incorrect instructions in the chip.
• **Hard disk fragmentation** happens when the data on your hard disk* gets disorganized. It can be tidied up by **defragging** - using a **defragmentation program** to sort out the data.
• **Corrupt disk** A damaged disk (either hard or floppy*) that doesn't work properly.

Computer crime

There are several kinds of **computer crime**. **Computer theft** is common, because computers are very valuable. A **chip heist** is a burglary where chips* are stolen from inside computers. **Computer fraud** means changing data in a computer, for example to cover up crimes such as embezzlement (stealing money from a company you work for). **Spoofing** means

trying to sabotage (damage) data by deliberately making a computer system* go wrong.

Measures to prevent theft and fraud are called **computer security**. A **case lock** locks the case* of your computer. A **disk drive lock** locks your disk drive* so no one else can use it. A **removable hard disk*** can be taken out of your computer and locked away to keep data safe.

Disk drive lock

Software* **piracy** means copying (or **pirating**) a piece of software to use or sell. To prevent pirating, some software companies supply a **dongle**, a plug which fits into the back of the computer. The software will only work when its dongle is in place, so pirated copies are not much use.

Dongle

Hacking

A **hacker** is a person who tries to **hack into** or **break into** (gain entry to) computers, to look at, change or destroy data. This is usually done by **cracking** (finding) the password* that protects the data on a computer. Hackers are sometimes called **electronic outlaws** or **electronic terrorists**.

Data can be **encrypted** (written in code) so that hackers can't make sense of it, and then **decrypted** (decoded) when it is needed. **Data protection** means trying to keep data safe from hackers and other criminals.

 *Backing up, 23; Bug, 37; Case, 12; Chip, 21; Computer system, 4; Disk drive, 23; Floppy disk, 23; Function, 4; Hard disk, 23; Hardware, 4; Keyboard, 6; Mouse, 7; Password, 18; Program, 36; Software, 4, 24

🖳 Viruses

A **computer virus** is a *program** which can attach itself to other programs and reproduce itself, spreading from one computer to another through a *network** or on *floppy disks**. Viruses are written deliberately by criminals called **virus-writers** to damage data, or just to annoy people.

Viruses can make strange things happen to your data, or write messages on your screen.

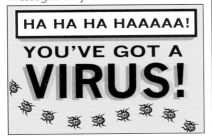

Some viruses (**joke viruses**) are harmless, but some can destroy all your data. Some, such as the **Queeg virus**, leave a rude message on the screen. Famous viruses include the **Michelangelo virus**, the **Maltese Amoeba** and the **Jerusalem virus**, which all destroy, or **trash**, data, and the **Cascade virus**, which makes the *characters** on the screen fall into a heap at the bottom.

Here are some types of virus:
- **Trojan horse** or **Trojan** A virus that gets into a computer by disguising itself as another, safer, program.
- **Worm** A virus which can reproduce itself independently, without having to attach itself to other programs.
- **Logic bomb** A virus which is activated when a particular program is *running**. A **time bomb** is a virus that only affects a computer on a certain date.
- **Intended virus** A virus that doesn't work as it was meant to.

A computer that is affected, or **infected**, by a virus is called a **host**. **Anti-virus programs** (or **vaccines**) and **virus checking programs** can make computers safe from, or **immune** to, some types of virus.

*Some anti-virus programs, such as **Norton Utilities Disk Doctor**, show graphics* on the screen while they are running.*

⚠ User safety

Using a computer for a long period of time can be bad for you. Sitting in a bad position can give you back-ache or neck ache, and light reflecting off the screen (called *glare**) could hurt your eyes.

Injuries to the wrists and hands can be caused by using the *keyboard** and *mouse**. These include **Repetitive Strain Injury** or **RSI**, often caused by typing, and

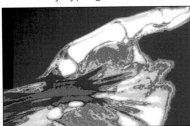

Scan of a hand affected by carpal tunnel syndrome. Blue and pink show inflamed, painful areas.

tendinitis, **tenosynovitis** and **carpal tunnel syndrome**, which are inflammations of the tendons leading to your fingers.

To avoid injury, you should take a regular 10-minute break, or **screen break**, every hour, shake your hands and wrists and

Ergonomic keyboard

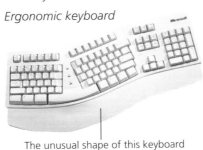

The unusual shape of this keyboard makes it very comfortable to use.

Foot rest

You can change the angle of the foot rest.

Your feet rest flat on this non-slip surface.

look around the room. Safety equipment such as **wrist rests** and **foot rests** can help you sit in a safe position, and an *ergonomic** or **hand-shaped mouse** and **ergonomic keyboard** can help reduce strain.

Mouse mat with a built-in wrist rest

Your wrist rests on here.

Hand-shaped mouse

Your fingers fit in these grooves.

**Character, 6; Ergonomic mouse, 7; Floppy disk, 23; Glare, 7; Graphics, 30; Keyboard, 6; Mouse, 7; Network, 18, 42; Program, 36; Running, 24*

Living with computers

The number of computers in the world is rising rapidly. In the last twenty years, computers have changed the way we do all sorts of everyday things, such as shopping, working and finding out information. These changes are often referred to as the **computer revolution**, the **digital revolution**, or the **information technology** (or **infotech**) **revolution**. People who have grown up with computers are often called the **digital generation**.

Computers are often used in schools.

The word "**cyber**", which comes from the Greek word *kubernan* meaning "to control", often appears in computer words. For example, **cyber-culture** means computer culture, a **cyber-society** means a

An animatronic dinosaur from a museum exhibition

computerized* society, and **cyberskills** are computer skills.

If you understand computers, you are **computer literate** or **computerate**. **Cyberphobia** is a fear of computers, and **technophobia** means fear of anything technological. These fears can sometimes stop people using computers, and are known as the **FUD** (**Fear, Uncertainty and Doubt**) **factor**.

Information

Computer technology is often called **Information Technology** (**IT**) because computers have had such a big effect on the way information is stored and spread.

The media (such as television, newspapers and magazines) is one of the main areas to be affected. **Online media** or **paperless media** means using a computer *network** as a kind of media. For example, **online newspapers** can be sent straight to your screen instead of printed on paper. **TV on demand** or **video on demand systems** let you choose a film or programme to watch, which is then sent to your television over a network. Videos can also be stored on *CDs** called **video CDs**, and played on a **video CD player** linked to your television.

Museums often use computers to make exhibits more exciting. **Animatronics** means using computers to control *robots**. It is used to make moving exhibits showing animals or machines.

Information once stored in books can now be kept in a **virtual library** or **electronic library**, stored on *CD-ROMs**. Writers have also used CD-ROMs for *hypertext** **novels**. You can read the pages of a hypertext novel in any order, so the story is different every time.

Jobs

Many people now work from home, using computer *networks** to link themselves to their workplace. This is called **telecommuting** or **tele-working**. A **telecottage** or **telecentre** is a local centre where people share the use of computers, *fax** machines and other equipment which helps them telecommute.

This woman is telecommuting using a notebook computer.*

The digital revolution has also created lots of new jobs. As well as computer *programmers** and engineers, companies need people called **IT** (Information Technology - see left) **trainers** or **IT instructors** to teach their employees how to use computers. To create products such as *CD-ROMs**, specially skilled *multimedia** **authors** and **multimedia designers** are needed. You might find a job like this in **online postings** - job advertisements which you can find on the *Internet**.

---

*CD, 23; CD-ROM, 35; Computerized, 4; Fax, 19; Hypertext, 35; Internet, 42; Multimedia, 35; Network, 18, 42; Notebook, 13; Programmer, 36; Robot, 15

Clever inventions

Computers are being used to help disabled people in various ways. A **videophone** uses a computer *network** to link two screens together, so that deaf people can see each other using sign language on the telephone. This is called **computer-telephony** or **video-telephony**.

A **functional electronic stimulus system** is being developed which can help paralyzed people walk. The system stimulates the muscles with electrical signals, so they can make walking movements.

A man using a computerized stimulus system to help him walk

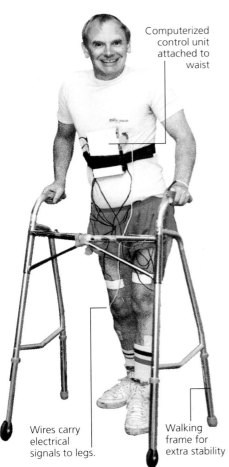

Computerized control unit attached to waist

Wires carry electrical signals to legs.

Walking frame for extra stability

Shopping

Computers are being used to make choosing and paying for shopping easier. Computerized *EFTPOS** systems let you pay for goods using **payment cards**, such as **direct debit cards**, which transfer money straight from your bank account. Another kind of card is a **smart card**.

A smart card cut-away to show the chip* inside

Computer-processed photo of card holder

S C

Supershop Smart Card Scheme

Al Gorithm

A chip inside the card stores information.

The card is thicker than a normal payment card.

A smart card can store units of value and other information. You can "**charge up**" your card by paying to have units put on it, and then use it to pay for things. Some shops use smart cards called **loyalty cards**, which store information about what you have bought and how much you have spent. The shop's computer can read this data from the card and give you discounts. This is called a **loyalty scheme**.

Many shops use a *computerized* barcode scanner** to read the price of an item. Some shops have **self-scanning**. You scan the things yourself, and an extra scanner spots anything you miss out.

A system called a **tagging** system can even read the price of everything in a trolley or basket without you having to take the things out, by tagging the items with labels called **passive radiant tags**.

Some shops have **in-store touchscreens*** and *multimedia** **systems** to give you information - for example, to show you a map of the store or print out a recipe.

Home shopping, also called **virtual shopping** or **online shopping**, is another way to buy goods, using a television or a computer connected to a *network**. You choose from a range of items on the screen. With some clothes shopping systems, you can see the clothes *composited** onto a photo of yourself, to see how they would look. This is called a **virtual mirror**. Catalogues of goods, or **virtual catalogues**, can be sent to you on *CD**.

A kind of computer called an **HHCT** (**Hand-Held Computer Terminal**) can be used in shops and restaurants. For example, a waiter might take your order, type it into his HHCT, and transmit it instantly to a computer *printer** in the kitchen.

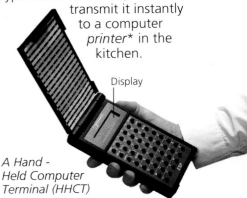

Display

A Hand - Held Computer Terminal (HHCT)

*Barcode scanner, 6; CD, 23; Chip, 21; Compositing, 31; Computerized, 4; EFTPOS, 15; Multimedia, 35; Network, 18, 42; Printer, 10; Touchscreen, 15

The Internet

The **Internet**, also known as the **Net**, is a worldwide computer *network** made up of smaller networks. It offers various services, or **Internet facilities**, to anyone who is connected to it, or "**on the Net**". You can use the Net to send letters, talk to friends, copy *files** and *software** from other computers, and look up information from sources all over the world. **Cyberspace** means the imaginary space you travel around in when you use the Net. Even though you stay in one place, you make a "**virtual journey**" around the world by linking up to different places.

The Internet grew out of an American military network called **DARPANET** (**Defence Advanced Research Projects Agency NETwork**), which was then changed to **ARPANET**. This proved to be so useful that a new network, **NSFNET** (**National Science Foundation NETwork**) was created for research and educational organizations to use. By 1990, anyone could join, and the Internet was born. The Net is not strictly controlled, but the NSF recommends a set of rules for users, called the **acceptable use policy**.

This diagram shows the main connections on the NSFNET on a map of the USA.

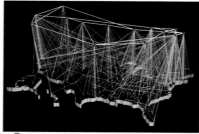

 Connections

Any computer that is connected to the Internet is known as a **host**, and a network (a *LAN** or *WAN**) connected to the Net is called a **site**. Some sites, especially government and university networks, have a **dedicated connection**. This is a permanent connection - the site is linked to the Net all the time.

If you are not on a dedicated connection, you can join or **hook up** to the Net by paying a company called a **service provider** to connect you. You can be connected in various ways:

• **Dial-in connection** This means the company has a direct link to the Internet. Using a *modem** or *ISDN** adaptor, you dial in and use their connection.

• **Dial-up** or **terminal connection** With this type of connection, you connect to a company that does not have a direct link. Instead, their network is connected to the Net through a *computer system** called a **gateway**.

• **Mail-only connection** A connection you can only use for email (see right).

Data is transmitted over the Net using **protocols**, such as **TCP/IP** (**Transmission Control Protocol/Internet**

Protocol). A protocol is a way of splitting data into chunks called **data packets**, or enclosing it in pieces of electronic code called "**envelopes**", so it travels safely to the right place.

 Email

Email, sometimes spelt **e-mail,** is short for **electronic mail** - sending messages on the Internet. Most people use email to send letters more cheaply and quickly than "**snail mail**", or normal mail. You can also email *graphics**, *sound** and even video, using a system called **MIME** (**Multi-purpose Internet Mail Extensions**).

Each person on the Internet has an **email address** for sending and receiving email. This consists of a **username** (the person's name), followed by an **@** symbol (which means "at"), followed by the address. The address usually shows the country, and the **domain** or **subdomain**, the place where the person can be found. There may also be a code showing the type of site (see left), such as **co** or **com** (a commercial site), **edu** or **ac** (academic), **gov** (government), or **org** (an organization).

An imaginary email address

anna@usborne.co.uk
Username Domain Code Country

An **email header** is a piece of technical information at the top of an email message, showing what route the message has taken. If an email **bounces**, or fails to get through, it is sent back to you, and you can look at the header to see what went wrong. An **online directory** is a computer list of email addresses.

---

*Computer system, 4; File, 25; Graphics, 30; ISDN, 45; LAN, 18; Modem, 19; Network, 18, 42; Software, 4, 24; Sound, 32; WAN, 18

Meeting places

Many people use the Internet to get in touch with people with the same interests, or to find out about particular subjects, through **discussion groups** or **special interest groups**. The main system for doing this is **Usenet** (also called **Network News**). It has lots of groups, or **newsgroups**, for all sorts of interests and hobbies.

You can "go to" a newsgroup by entering its name on your computer. Newsgroups are all named according to their subjects, called **topics** and **subtopics**. Topics include **comp** (computers), **sci** (science), **soc** (social groups), **rec** (recreation) and **alt** (alternative groups).

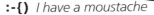

An imaginary name for a newsgroup about frogs

sci.bio.frogs

Topic | Subtopics

In a newsgroup, you can write, or **post**, messages and then see other people's answers, called **followups**, appear on your screen. Lots of people can take part at once. **Flaming**, or sending **flame mail**, means sending angry messages. A **flame war** is an argument.

Most newsgroups have a **FAQ** (**Frequently Asked Questions**) message for new members to read. This saves the other members having to answer the same questions again and again.

Smileys (often spelt **smilies**), or **emoticons**, are little pictures made up from *characters** on the *keyboard**. They can be used to add emotions or extra meanings to your newsgroup messages. Here are some smileys. (You have to look at them sideways.)

:-) *Happy/sarcastic*
:-D *Laughing*
:-(*Sad/angry*
:-O *Surprised*
I-O *Bored*
:-{} *I have a moustache*

You can use email (see facing page), to take part in a kind of discussion group called a **mailing list**. All the members of the group put their addresses in a list. They can then write email messages which are sent to everyone on the list. Each mailing list is run by a person, or by a *program** called a **listserv**.

World Wide Web

The **World Wide Web**, also called **WWW** or the **Web**, is an Internet facility (see facing page) that lets you find information from all over the world. It is so powerful that it is nicknamed the "**killer application**".

Web pages (information *documents** on the Web) are *hypertext**-**linked**. This means that some words are highlighted, and when you *click** on them with a *mouse** the Web takes you to a different "page" showing more information about that subject. This is done using a *program** called a **browser** or **Web browser**, such as **Mosaic** or **Cello**. Eventually, all the information on the Internet may be linked together on the Web.

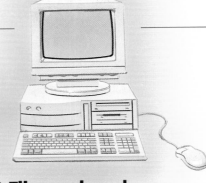

Files and gophers

Ftp (**file transfer protocol**) is the system you use to *download**, or copy, *files** from another computer onto your own, over the Internet. An **ftp site** is a site (see facing page) where files are available for downloading. You often need permission or **authorized access** to download a file, but there are lots of **anonymous ftp sites**, where files are freely available to anyone.

Finding ftp sites is complicated, so there are *programs** called **gophers** (named after a kind of animal) to help you. The main gopher is called **Archie**. When you give Archie a word (such as "frog"), it searches the whole of "**gopherspace**" (all over the Net) and gives you a list of sites. There are also other gophers, called **Veronica** and **Jughead**.

WOW!

Veronica and Jughead are named after characters from the American "Archie" comics. This picture shows Veronica.

---

*Character, 6; Clicking, 7; Document, 25; Downloading, 19; File, 25; Hypertext, 35;
Keyboard, 6; Mouse, 7; Program, 36

The history of computers

A computer really means a machine that helps you to do calculations. Simple counting machines, such as the **abacus**, have existed for thousands of years. However, the development of complicated modern computers, like the ones in this book, did not really begin until the nineteenth century. This time chart shows the most important dates.

An abacus is made from moving beads arranged on rods.

1833-4 The mathematician Charles *Babbage** started work on his **Analytical Engine**, the forerunner of the modern computer. It was mechanical and used punched cards, cogs and wheels instead of electronic signals. Babbage was helped by another mathematician called **Ada Augusta, Countess Lovelace**.

Ada Lovelace

Charles Babbage's Analytical Engine, which was only completed after his death.

1930-40 Punched card computers were widely used for doing large calculations. They all used **decimal code**, the counting system which uses the digits 0-9.

1937 A British mathematician called **Alan Turing** invented a theoretical design for a computer, known as the **Turing machine**. This was used during the later development of computers.

1941 A German scientist, **Konrad Zuse**, built the first computer to use *binary**.

1945 The first completely electronic computer, **ENIAC** (**Electronic Numeric Integrator And Calculator**), was built by **Presper Eckert** and **John Mauchly** for the US Army.

1947 The *transistor** was invented. Early transistors were bigger than modern ones, and got very hot.

1948 The **Manchester University Mark I**, the first computer able to store *programs**, was completed.

1951 The **Ferranti Mark I**, an improved version of the Manchester University Mark I, went on sale.

An early transistor

1960 The first silicon *chips** were produced. This made it possible to build much smaller computers.

1964 The first computers built using silicon chips went on sale.

1975 The first small home computer, the **Altair**, was sold. The *software** company **Microsoft** was founded in the USA by **Bill Gates** and **Paul Allen**.

Silicon chip

1976 A new computer company, Apple Computer, was founded in the USA by **Steve Jobs** and **Steve Wozniak**. **Apple 1**, Apple's first computer, was built and went on sale.

1980 The **Sharp PC 1211**, the first *portable**, was launched.

Sharp PC 1211

1981 **IBM** (**International Business Machines**) introduced the *IBM PC**, a model that set the standard in small computers for the next few years. Microsoft brought out *MS-DOS**, an operating system (*OS**) for use with IBM PCs.

1982 The electronics company *Intel** produced its 286 chip.

1983 Microsoft introduced the *Microsoft Windows** operating system.

1984 Apple introduced the Apple Macintosh (*Mac**), a computer built to rival the IBM PC.

1985 Intel released its 386 chip.

1986 Author **William Gibson** invented the word *cyberspace** in his novel *Neuromancer*.

1989 Intel 486 chip appeared.

1991 Apple, IBM and a company called Motorola announced a partnership to develop the **Power PC chip**. This enabled IBM and Apple computers to use the same software.

William Gibson

1993 Intel introduced the Pentium processor™ chip.

1994 Apple and IBM launched the *Power Mac** and *Power PC**.

1995 Microsoft launched the **Windows 95** operating system.

*Babbage, 14; Binary, 20; Chip, 21; Cyberspace, 42; IBM PC, 12; Intel, 12; Mac, 12; Microsoft Windows, 26; MS-DOS, 24; OS, 24; Portables, 13; Power Mac, 12; Power PC, 12; Program, 36; Software, 4, 24; Transistor, 21

The future

Although computers have revolutionized the world, there are lots more changes to come. Nobody knows exactly what will happen as computers become more powerful. Some amazing inventions are being developed. Others are still just ideas.

Communication

Lots more people will join the *Internet**, making communication much easier. The phrases **global village** and **digital community** describe a world where everyone is linked together by computers. Using the Internet, everyone will be able to find information easily.

Information will travel much faster than it does now. A new *network** called **ISDN** (**Integrated Services Digital Network**) will replace telephone wires with **digital telephone lines**, which carry data in a *digital** form using a very high *bandwidth**. A device called an **ISDN adaptor** will be used instead of a *modem**.

Soon, you will also be able to buy a **telecomputer**, or **teleputer**, a machine which is a television, a computer and a telephone all in one.

Intelligence

Scientists are researching ways to make computers think like human beings. This is called **AI** or **Artificial Intelligence**. AI scientists often use specially designed *programming languages**, such as **Lisp**.

Neural networks or **neural nets** are computers or *programs** that are designed to work like the human brain. **Fuzzy logic** means a computer can recognize a range, or **fuzzy set**, of different levels of certainty. Instead of understanding only "true" and "false", the computer can make value judgements, more like a person does.

Using a combination of AI and advanced engineering techniques, scientists may eventually create truly lifelike **androids** - *robots** that look and behave like humans. There are already some androids, but they are not completely realistic.

This android, called "Manny", was built by the USA government for testing safety clothing.

The android can *simulate** sweating and breathing.

The android's movements can be very precise. They are controlled by a computer.

Hydraulic (fluid-pressured) engine sytems make parts of the android move.

Manny is "fully articulated", which means his joints can move just like a person's.

Electrical signals are sent around the android's "body" along wires.

Virtual life

Virtual Reality* (VR) is already being used in lots of ways - for example, in medicine, entertainment and design. But VR is not yet very realistic. As techniques improve, though, VR could seem so real that you could live a **virtual life** - having most of your experiences through VR. **Virtual travel systems** could take you on a **virtual holiday**, letting you experience other parts of the world through a *VR headset**. Even further into the future, people might one day be able to travel digitally, or **teleport**, from place to place, instead of having to move around physically.

Some people even think that VR headsets might be replaced by a **DNI** (**Direct Neural Interface**) that would plug straight into your brain, and stimulate your brain cells to give you a **virtual experience**. A **brain implant** would work in a similar way, but would give you special skills, like being able to speak a new language or play an instrument, without you having to learn it.

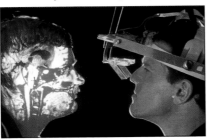

A scientist using Virtual Reality to "explore" a simulation* of the human brain.

*Bandwidth, 19; Digital, 4, 19; Internet, 42; Modem, 19; Network, 18, 42; Program, 36; Programming language, 36; Robot, 15; Simulation, 28; Virtual Reality, 34; VR headset, 34

Glossary of computer slang

 Internet slang

There is a lot of **Net slang**, or slang words connected with the *Internet**. These are changing and growing in number all the time, but some of the most common ones are listed here.

Electronic anarchy The state of freedom and lawlessness that exists on the Internet. There are few rules and restrictions, so you can do and say what you like.

Electrotransvestism Pretending to be a member of the opposite sex when sending Internet messages.

E-zine A magazine available over the Internet in the form of electronic data.

Infobahn, Information superhighway Slang words for the Internet.

Lurking Reading the messages of a *newsgroup** without sending any yourself. This is one way to find out about a group.

Net cop or **Net judge** Someone who thinks they can tell other Internet users how to behave, according to the rules of netiquette (see right).

Net cult A *newsgroup** or other group representing "cult" interests, such as witchcraft, magic or drugs.

Net evangelist Someone who tries to persuade other people to use the Internet.

Net surfing or **surfing on the net** Exploring the Internet. So called because when you use the Net, your computer equipment sometimes makes a fuzzy sound that sounds a bit like the sea.

Net traffic Data moving around on the Internet.

Net users People who use the Internet. There are many other words for this, including

netters, **netsters**, **netizens** or **net citizens**, **netheads**, the **netoisie**, **internauts** and **infonauts**.

Netiquette The rules of polite behaviour, which you should keep to when using the Internet.

Netzine A magazine all about the Internet.

Newbie A new Internet user or a new member of a *newsgroup**.

Newbie hunting Searching for newbies who aren't sure what they're doing, and teasing them.

Noise Ongoing conversation or chat in a *newsgroup**, especially conversation which is not very relevant to the topic of the newsgroup.

Rodent Slang for *gopher**. See also "Other slang".

Shouting Writing messages in CAPITAL LETTERS to show you are in a bad mood.

Spamming Sending junk *email**, especially when done deliberately to annoy someone.

Virtual relationship A friendship or relationship that starts on the Internet. Meeting someone face to face whom you have first made contact with on the Internet is called **boinking**.

 Other slang

Computer-friendly Willing to use and learn about computers.

Computerholic Addicted to computers, or a person who is addicted to using their computer.

Core wars A game played by computer *programmers**, in which each player tries to write a *program** that will destroy the other player's program.

Cyberzine A magazine about computers and computing.

Eat up To use up a lot of *processing power** or *RAM**. Some *software** does this.

Front end This means the place where a user is when using a computer, especially when connected to a *network**.

Gulp A group of more than eight *bits** (so called because it is bigger than a *byte**).

Junking or **binning** *Deleting** something from a computer.

Liveware A computer slang word for people. Also called **wetware** or **the meat**.

Lunchbox A name for a *notebook** computer.

Mouse potato Someone who sits in front of a computer all day. This comes from "couch potato" - someone who watches television all day.

Nerd or **computer nerd** A rude word for someone who is obsessed with computers. A nerd can also be called a **geek**, a **dweeb**, an **anorak** or a **propeller head** (because in the US, computer nerds used to wear caps with spinning propellers on top).

Nybble A group of less than eight *bits** (so called because it is smaller than a *byte**).

Power-hungry Needing a lot of *processing power**.

Rodent A *mouse**. See also "Internet slang".

Show-stopper A computer fault or problem that stops a system from working.

Superhighwayman Another name for a *hacker**.

Techie Someone who knows about the more technical aspects of computers.

Vapourware *Software** that exists only as an idea and hasn't yet been invented.

Wired Feeling funny from having spent too long staring at a computer screen. "Wired" can also mean connected to a *network** or to the *Internet**.

*Bit, 20; Byte, 20; Deleting, 25; Email, 42; Gopher, 43; Hacker, 38; Internet, 42; Mouse, 7; Network, 18, 42; Newsgroup, 43; Notebook, 13; Processing power, 9; Program(mer), 36; RAM, 22; Software, 4, 24

Glossary of acronyms

This list provides a quick guide to some of the more common computer-related acronyms. The numbers show the page on which each acronym is explained. Some of the acronyms explained here do not appear anywhere else in the book.

AD Analog-Digital (converter) **32**
ALU Arithmetic Logic Unit **9**
ARPANET Advanced Research Projects Agency NETwork **42**
BBS Bulletin Board System **19**
BIOS Basic Input/Output System **9**
bps bits per second **19**
CAD Computer-Aided Design **29**
CAM Computer-Aided Manufacturing **15**
CAT Computer-Aided Testing **29**
CAT Computerized Axial Tomography (scanner) **15**
CD Compact Disc **23**
CD-i Compact Disc-interactive **48**
CD-ROM Compact Disc-Read-Only Memory **35**
CGI Computer-Generated Imagery **30**
CISC Complex Instruction Set Computer (CPU) **21**
CMOS Complementary Metal Oxide Semiconductor (RAM) **22**
cps characters per second **11**
CPU Central Processing Unit **9**
CRT Cathode Ray Tube (monitor) **7**
DA Digital-Analog (converter) **32**
DAP Digital Audio Processing **32**
DARPANET Defence Advanced Research Projects Agency NETwork **42**
DAT Digital Audio Tape **33**
DBMS DataBase Management System **27**
DCC Digital Compact Cassette **33**
DIP Digital Image Processing **30**
DNI Direct Neural Interface **45**
DOS Disk Operating System **24**
DP Data Processing (department) **14**
dpi dots per inch **11**

DRAM Dynamic RAM **22**
DTP DeskTop Publishing **28**
EFTPOS Electronic Funds Transfer at Point Of Sale **15**
EISA Extended Industry Standard Architecture (bus) **20**
ENIAC Electronic Numeric Integrator And Calculator **44**
EPROM Erasable Programmable ROM **22**
FAQ Frequently Asked Questions **43**
FLOPS FLoating point Operations Per Second **21**
FPS File Processing System **27**
Ftp File transfer protocol **43**
FUD Fear, Uncertainty and Doubt (factor) **40**
GB Gigabyte **22**
GUI Graphical User Interface **24**
HHCT Hand-Held Computer Terminal **41**
IBM International Business Machines **44**
IC Integrated Circuit **21**
IP Internet Protocol **42**
IRCAM Institut de Recherche et de Coordination Acoustique/Musique **33**
ISA Industry Standard Architecture (bus) **20**
ISDN Integrated Services Digital Network **45**
IT Information Technology **40**
JANET Joint Academic NETwork. A *network** which connects universities and colleges in the UK, and forms part of the *Internet**.
LAN Local Area Network **18**
LCD Liquid Crystal Display **13**
LED Light-Emitting Diode **7**
MB Megabyte **22**
MCA Micro Channel Architecture (bus) **20**
MIDI Musical Instrument Digital Interface **32**
MIME Multi-purpose Internet Mail Extensions **42**
MIPS Millions of Instructions Per Second **21**

MPEG Motion Pictures Experts Group (compression) **48**
MS-DOS Microsoft Disk Operating System **24**
NSFNET National Science Foundation NETwork **42**
OCR Optical Character Recognition (scanner) **16**
OS Operating System **24**
PAD Packet Assembler and Disassembler **19**
PC Personal Computer **4, 12**
PCB Printed Circuit Board **8**
PCI Peripheral Component Interconnect (local bus) **20**
PCMCIA Personal Computer Memory Cards International Association (expansion card) **20**
ppm pages per minute **11**
RAM Random-Access Memory **22**
RISC Reduced Instruction Set Computer (CPU) **21**
ROM Read-Only Memory **22**
RSI Repetitive Strain Injury **39**
SCSI Small Computer Systems Interface **23**
SIMMs Single In-line Memory Modules **22**
SLOC Source Lines Of Code **37**
SQA Software Quality Assurance **37**
SVGA Super Video Graphics Array **7**
TCP Transmission Control Protocol **42**
TLA Three-Letter Acronym
UI User Interface **24**
VDU Visual Display Unit **7**
VESA Video Electronics Standard Association (local bus) **20**
VGA Video Graphics Array **7**
VR Virtual Reality **34**
WAIS Wide Area Information Service. A huge collection of information available to anyone using the *Internet**.
WAN Wide Area Network **18**
WP Word Processing **26**
WWW World Wide Web **43**
WYSIWYG What You See Is What You Get **26**

*Internet, 42; Network, 18, 42

Glossary of extra words

This glossary contains some extra computer words you might come across which do not appear in the rest of the book.

Acoustic coupler A device used instead of a *modem** to connect a computer to a telephone line. It is attached to the telephone handset, so it can easily be used in public telephone boxes, and is useful away from the home or office.

Bells and whistles Noises that are part of a piece of *software**, or any special extras or gimmicks that are sold with computer equipment.

Bernoulli drive A very fast kind of *disk drive** which uses special flexible disks. The disks are held in the right place by the drive's spinning action.

Board Another name for an *expansion card**.

Boolean algebra A mathematical system which allows facts to be expressed as either "true" or "false" (the basis of computer language).

Broadband A cable or channel that can carry a large amount of data at once.

CD-i (Compact Disc-interactive) A kind of compact disc (*CD**), similar to a *CD-ROM**, but which works with a television instead of with a computer. CD-i discs need a special CD-i player which plugs into the TV. Like CD-ROMs, CD-i discs are used for both entertainment and education.

Colour thermal printer A colour *printer** that works by applying heat to specially coated paper.

Cyberguru A person who is famous in the world of computers, especially in relation to the *Internet**.

Daisy chain To link computers or other computer equipment together in series (in a chain) instead of in a ring or star shape, which is more common.

Data highway Another name for a *bus**. Buses are also known as **highways** and **trunks**, especially in the US.

Default An automatic setting often found in *software**. If you do not make a choice from a range of options, the computer will choose the default setting.

Digital rights or **electronic rights** Legal rights, such as copyright, relating to material that is created and stored using computer equipment.

Enhance or **computer-enhance** To improve something, especially pictures or sounds, using computers. For example, telescope pictures of outer space are often enhanced, or made easier to see, using **enhancement** *software**.

Geographical Information Systems (GIS) *Software** that is used to make and analyze maps and plans.

Glitch A *bug**, mistake or defect in a computer.

Invisible effects Using special *software** to remove unwanted bits from films. For example, you could film an actor "flying" on safety wires, and then remove the wires from the picture using a computer.

Keystroke The act of pressing one key on the *keyboard**.

Kilobaud A unit used to measure how fast data can travel along a cable or channel.

Logging Gaining access to a *network** or a computer, especially a *mainframe**, is called **logging in** or **logging on**. When you finish using the system, you **log out** or **log off**.

Macro A small *program**, or set of instructions. Many types of *software** allow the user to write macros to help save time. You can carry out, or **invoke**, a macro with just a couple of keystrokes (see left). Then it runs through all its instructions without any more keystrokes.

Mailbase A list of addresses for a particular special interest group on the *Internet**.

Mechatronics A combination of mechanics and electronics, often used in building computerized machines.

MPEG (Motion Pictures Experts Group) compression A method used to *compress** video data, so that it can be stored on *CDs**. There are two versions - **MPEG1** and **MPEG2**.

Multi-user games *Games** in which you can play against several other people, linked together on the *Internet**. Many of these are adventure games known as **Multi-User Dungeon (MUD) games**.

Natural language interface A *program** which lets the user give the computer instructions using natural language (the person's own natural way of expressing things) instead of specific words.

Near-zero footprint A phrase often used in advertisements to describe a piece of equipment that takes up hardly any space on a desk or table.

Object-Oriented Programming (OOP) A method of *programming**. The programmer writes several shorter programs, called **objects**. Instead of containing just instructions, each object can contain both instructions and data. The objects then work together to run the program.

*Bug, 37; Bus, 20; CD, 23; CD-ROM, 35; Compression, 23; Disk drive, 23; Expansion card, 8; Games, 34; Internet, 42; Keyboard, 6; Mainframe, 14; Modem, 19; Network, 18, 42; Printer, 10; Program(ming), 36; Software, 4, 24

Online democracy A possible development in the future, which would allow people to take part in political debates, talk to the government, and even vote, using the *Internet**.

Online tutorial A lesson over the *Internet**, especially one that teaches someone how to use the Internet itself.

Parity A system which prevents data being corrupted (damaged) when it is being sent along electronic pathways inside a computer, or along cables to another piece of *hardware**.

Park When you move a computer, the *hard disk** can get scratched and damaged by its moving parts. To keep the disk safe, you **park** it using a *program** that prevents these parts from moving.

Personal information manager A piece of *software** that helps people organize their time and make lists of things to do and people to see. Also called a **contact manager**.

Phase diffusion or **spatial processing** Using a type of *software** to make 3-D music that surrounds an audience. It works by giving out sounds at fractionally different times from several different loudspeakers.

PKzip software or **PKware** A group of public domain (see below) *programs** used for *compressing** data.

Public domain *Software** that is available for anyone to use and that costs nothing. It is usually found on the *Internet**.

Robotic prosthetic A computer-controlled artificial limb or other artificial body part.

Router A computer that handles and redirects messages and other data that are being sent over a large *network**.

Simplex modem A type of *modem** that can only send data in one direction.

Soft A word used to describe computer equipment or processes that can be changed using *software**. For example, a **soft key** is a key that can have different purposes, depending on what software is being used. A **soft boot** means stopping and restarting your computer without switching it off.

Speaker-independent voice recognition A system that can understand anyone that speaks to it, just as a person can. This is still being developed.

Systems operator or **sysop** Someone who organizes and runs a service such as a Bulletin Board System (*BBS**).

TAN (**Total Area Network**) Any *network** that extends all over the world.

Tape streamer A *tape drive** which can be used to make a copy of everything on a computer's *hard disk**.

Telepresence A system which uses a *network** and specially designed *software** to make you feel as if you are somewhere you are not. This is used in **telesurgery** which allows surgeons to operate on someone who is a long way away from them. The surgeon sees a video of the patient, and uses special controls to send instructions to a very advanced *robot** which carries out the operation.

Telnet A facility on the *Internet** which lets you use another person's computer. Often used for playing multi-user games (see facing page).

Throughput The amount of work a computer or other piece of *hardware** can do in a given amount of time.

Touchtone phone A telephone which sends sound signals, or tones, when the buttons are pressed. The signals can be received by a computer. You can use a touchtone phone to order goods or book tickets (called **touchtone booking**) directly from a computer linked to the telephone system, without speaking to a real person.

Translation system *Software** that can translate a piece of writing from one language into another. This has not been fully developed, but it could eventually be used to help people communicate on the *Internet** and in other ways.

Transputer A type of computer which can process more than one piece of data at once. Transputers are not used very much because they are very difficult to write *programs** for. They are still being developed.

True colour monitor A *monitor** that can show the complete range of colours visible to people - over 16.4 million colours.

V32bis A standard type of *modem**. A V32bis modem can transmit 14,400 bits per second or *bps**. There are several other standard modem types. For example, a **V22bis modem** is slower than a V32bis, and a **Vfast modem** is faster.

Valves Parts which were used in computers before *transistors** were invented. Valves were larger and heavier than transistors, so computers had to be quite big too.

Wild card A symbol that can be used to stand for anything. The symbol ***** is often used as a wild card. For example, "*.txt" means any *file** that ends with the *extension** ".txt".

---

*BBS, 19; bps, 19; Compression, 23; Extension, 25; File, 25; Hard disk, 23; Hardware, 4; Internet, 42; Modem, 19; Monitor, 7; Network, 18, 42; Program, 36; Robot, 15; Software, 4, 24; Tape drive, 23; Transistor, 21; Virus, 39

Index

Numbers

2-D animation, multilayered, **31**
3.5 inch floppy disk, **23**
3-D animation, **31**
3-D mouse, **34**
3-D user interface, **24**
4GL (Fourth Generation Language), **36**
5.25 inch floppy disk, **23**
8-bit bus, 20
8-bit sound card, **32**
8 inch floppy disk, **23**
16-bit bus, **20**
16-bit sound card, **32**
32-bit bus, **20**
64-bit bus, 12, **20**
286, 9, **12**, 44
386, 9, **12**, 20, 44
486, 9, **12**, 44
68020, **12**
68030, **12**
68040, **12**
80486, Intel, **12**

A

abacus, **44**
ac (in an email address), **42**
access (to access a computer), **18**
access (to access parts of RAM), **22**
access, authorized, **43**
access time, **22**
accordion fold paper, **11**
acoustic coupler, **48**
acoustic model, **32**
acronyms, 47
action game, **34**
AD (Analog-Digital) converter, **32**, 47
Ada, **36**
adaptor,
      graphics, 7
      ISDN, 42, **45**
      mains, **13**
      modem, **19**
Adaptor, Peripheral Interface (PIA), **8**
address (in RAM), **22**
address (on a LAN), **18**
address, email, **42**
address bus, **20**
adventure game, **34**
aerial view function, **29**
AI (Artificial Intelligence), 36, **45**
algorithm, **37**
      flocking, **31**
algorithm library, **37**
alphanumeric key, **6**
alpha testing, **37**
alt (newsgroup topic), **43**
Altair, 12, **44**

ALU (Arithmetic Logic Unit), **9**, 47
ambient music, **33**
Analog-Digital (AD) converter, **32**, 47
analog signal, **19**, 32
analysis graphics, **30**
analyst, systems, 14, **36**
Analytical Engine, 14, **44**
and gate, **21**
android, **45**
animation, computer, **31**
animatronics, **40**
anonymous ftp site, **43**
anorak, **46**
anti-glare filter, **7**
anti-static mouse mat, **38**
anti-virus program, **39**
Apple 1, **44**
Apple Computer, **12**, 44
Apple Macintosh (Mac), 4, **12**, 44
applications, **24**, 25, 26, 28, 31, 36
      core or basic, **26**
applications development
      department, **36**
applications programmer, **36**
applications section, **14**
applications software, **24**
approach (programming), **37**
arcade game, **34**
Archie, **43**
architecture, **4**, 9, 12, 21
arithmetic, fixed point, **21**
arithmetic, floating point, **21**
Arithmetic Logic Unit (ALU), **9**, 47
ARPANET (Advanced Research
      Projects Agency NETwork),
      42, 47
array (in parallel processing), **14**
array (in RAM), **22**
art, computer, 17, **31**
Artificial Intelligence (AI), 36, **45**
assembler, **36**
AT bus, **20**
AT (chip), **12**
audio processing, **32**
authorized access, **43**
autobackup, **38**
autofire button, **16**
auto resume, **13**
autosave, **38**
autosensing power supply, **13**
auto suspend, **13**

B

Babbage, Charles, **14**, 44
BABT (British Approvals Board for
      Telecommunications), **19**
BABT-approved modem, **19**
back-up/backing up, **23**, 38

ballpoint mouse, **13**
bandwidth, **19**, 45
banking, 4, 40
barcode, **6**
barcode reader, **6**,
barcode scanner, **6**, 41
BASIC (Beginner's All-purpose
      Symbolic Instruction Code), **36**
basic applications, 26-27
Basic Input/Output System (BIOS), 8,
      9, 47
batteries, dual, **13**
battery,
      RAM, **22**
      Nickel Cadmium (NiCad), **13**
      Nickel Metal Hydryde (NiMH), **13**
battery pack, **13**
baud rate, **19**
BBC Computer, **12**
BBS (Bulletin Board System), **19**, 47, 49
bells and whistles, **48**
Bernoulli drive, **48**
beta tester, **37**
bi-directional printing, **11**
binary code, 17, **20**, 36, 44
binary digit, **20**
binning, **46**
BIOS (Basic Input/Output System), 8,
      9, 47
bit, 17, 19, **20**, 32, 46
bitmap, **11**
bitmapped graphics, **30**
bits per second (bps), **19**, 47
black (in printing), **10**
      registration, **10**
black and white printer, **10**
block, **26**
board, **48**
boinking, **46**
bold text, **26**
bomb, logic, **39**
bomb, time, **39**
book, electronic, **35**
Boolean algebra, **48**
booting up, **8**
Boulez, Pierre, 33
bouncing, **42**
bps (bits per second), **19**, 47
brain implant, **45**
breaking into (a computer), **38**
brightness button, **7**
British Approvals Board for
      Telecommunications (BABT), **19**
broadband, **48**
browser, **43**
brush, **30**
      pressure-sensitive, **30**
      user-definable, **30**
bubblejet printer, **10**

*Page numbers in bold type (eg **37**) show where to find the main explanation of a word or phrase.*

bucket, **22**
buffer, memory, **11**
bug, **37**, 38, 48
bug fixing, **37**
buggy chip, **38**
built-in printer, **10**
Bulletin Board System (BBS), **19**, 47, 49
bundle, **16**
      multimedia, 16, **35**
bundled software, **25**
burn-in, **38**
bus, 8, 12, **20**, 21, 47
      8-bit, 20
      16-bit, **20**
      32-bit, **20**
      64-bit, **20**
      address, **20**
      AT, **20**
      control, **20**
      data, **20**
      expansion, **20**
      ISA, **20**, 47
      local, **20**
      MCA, **20**, 47
      multiplexed, **20**
      PCI, **20**, 47
      VESA, **20**, 47
      VL-bus, **20**
business, 4, 27, 36
business accounting software, **27**
business software, **27**
bus interface unit, **9**
bus LAN, **18**
busy, **4**
butler in a box, **17**
button,
      autofire, **16**
      brightness, **7**
      contrast, **7**
      degauss, **7**
      fire, **16**
      monitor, 5
      mouse, 5, **7**
      reset, 5, **8**
      turbo, 5, **8**
byte, 17, **20**, 22, 46

C

C, **36**
C++, **36**
cable, 5, 6, 7, 10, **17**, 18, 19
      coaxial, **18**
      fibre optic, **18**
      keyboard, 5, 6
      mouse, 5, 7, 16
      parallel, **17**
      printer, 5, **10**
      serial, **17**

cache, 12, **22**
      disk, **23**
cache memory, 12, **22**
CAD (Computer-Aided Design), 15,
      25, **29**, 30, 47
calculated cell, **27**
CAM (Computer-Aided
      Manufacturing), **15**, 47
camera,
      digital, **17**
      digital video, 3, **17**
capacitor, **9**
capacitor (part of RAM), **22**
capacitor, RAM, **13**
CAPS LOCK key, **6**
card, **8**
      direct debit, **41**
      expansion, **8**, 13, 19, 20, 22, 30,
          32, 48
      graphics, **30**, 35
      loyalty, **41**
      memory, **13**
      modem, **19**
      payment, **41**
      smart, **41**
      sound, **32**, 35
      video, **30**
carpal tunnel syndrome, **39**
carriage return, **10**
carry-and-park portable, **13**
cartridge,
      data, **23**
      ink, **10**
      tape, 14, **23**
      toner, **10**, 11
Cascade virus, **39**
case, 4, 8, **12**, 15, 38
      desktop, **12**
case lock, **38**
cashless payment systems, **15**
CAT (Computer-Aided Testing), **29**,
      47
Cathode Ray Tube (CRT) monitor, **7**,
      13, 47
CAT (Computerized Axial
      Tomography) scanner, **15**, 47
CAT scan, **15**
CCD (Charge Coupled Device), **16**
CD (Compact Disc), **23**, 32, 33, 35,
      40, 41, 47
      video, **40**
CD (Compact Disc) drive, 5, **35**
CD-i (Compact Disc-interactive), 47,
      48
CD-quality sound, **32**
CD-ROM, 23, **35**, 40, 47
CD-ROM drive, 3, 8, **35**
cel, **31**
cell (in RAM), **22**

cell (in a spreadsheet), **27**
Cello, **43**
cell pointer, **27**
centralized computing, **14**
Central Processing Unit (CPU), 5, 8,
      9, 12, 14, 20, 21, 47
      CISC, **21**, 47
      RISC, **21**, 47
      user-removable, **12**
centre controls, **7**
CGI (Computer-Generated Imagery),
      30, 47
character, **6**, 10, 11, 28, 39, 43
character graphics, **30**
character printer, **10**
character recognition program, **13**
characters per second (cps), **11**, 47
charge (electrical), **11**
Charge Coupled Device (CCD), **16**
charge up (a smart card), **41**
chart, **30**
chassis, **12**
cheapernet, **18**
checkout, computerized, **15**
chip, 5, 8, 9, 12, 14, 20, **21**, 22, 32,
      38, 44
      buggy, **38**
      CPU, 12, 14
      Power PC, **12**
      RAM, 8, 12, 22
      ROM, 8, 22
      silicon, 3, **21**, 44
      synthesizer, **32**
chip heist, **38**
circuit, electrical, **8**, 21
CISC (Complex Instruction Set
      Computer) CPU, **21**, 47
clicking, **7**, 35, 43
clicking and dragging, **7**
clip-on trackball, 3, **13**
clock, 8, **9**, 21
clock cycle, **9**
clock cycles per second, **9**
clock doubling, **21**
clock rate, **9**
clock speed, **9**
clock speed indicator, 8, **9**
clone, IBM, **12**
closing (a file), **25**
CMOS (Complementary Metal Oxide
      Semiconductor) RAM, **22**, 47
co (in an email address), **42**
coaxial cable, **18**
COBOL (COmmon Business Oriented
      Language), **36**
code, **36**,
      binary, 17, **20**, 36, 44
      decimal, **44**
      machine, **36**

Page numbers in bold type (eg **37**) *show where to find the main explanation of a word or phrase.*   **51**

object, **36**
source, **36**, 37
coding, 37
collaborative learning, **35**
colour printer, **10**
colour scan, **16**
colour screen, **5**
colour thermal printer, **48**
column, 27
com (in an email address), **42**
.com (file extension), **25**
combat game, **34**
Commodore 64, **12**
comms, **18**
communications channel, **19**
communications satellite, **18**
community, digital, **45**
comp (newsgroup topic), **43**
Compact Disc (CD), **23**, 32, 33, 35,
40, 41, 47
video, **40**
Compact Disc (CD) drive, 5, 8, 35
Compact Disc-interactive (CD-i), 47,
48
compiler program, **36**
Complementary Metal Oxide
Semiconductor (CMOS) RAM,
22, 47
Complex Instruction Set Computer
(CISC) CPU, **21**, 47
component, **9**
compositing, **31**
video, **31**
compression (data), 19, **23**, 48, 49
computer, **4**
BBC, **12**
dedicated, **15**, 34
games, 15, **34**
general-purpose, **15**
home, **4**
IBM personal, **12**, 20, 44
personal, **4**, **12** (see also PC)
special-purpose, **15**
standalone, **18**
computer (as a name for the
processing unit), **8**
Computer-Aided Design (CAD), 15,
25, **29**, 30, 47
Computer-Aided Manufacturing
(CAM), **15**, 47
Computer-Aided Testing (CAT), **29**,
47
computer animation, **31**
computer art, 17, **31**
computer-assisted therapy, **15**
computerate, **40**
computer-coded ticket, **15**
computer consultancy, **36**
computer crime, **38**
computer failure, 38
computer fraud, **38**

computer-friendly, **46**
computer game, 3, 16, 25, 33, **34**,
35, 48
Computer-Generated Imagery (CGI),
30, 47
computer-generated sound, **32**
computer graphics, 5, 6, 7, 8, 10,
11, 18, 19, 25, 28, 30, 31,
33, **34**, 35, 39, 42 (see also
graphics software)
computerholic, **46**
computerized (machines), **4**, 6, 15, 33
Computerized Axial Tomography
(CAT) scanner, **15**, 47
computerized checkout, **15**
computerized public display, **6**
computer jargon, **3**
computer literate, **40**
computer nerd, **46**
computer operator, **14**
computer problems and solutions,
38-39
computer program, 4, 10, 13, 14,
15, 16, 19, 23, 24, 25, 26,
27, 31, 32, 33, **36**, 37, 38,
39, 43, 44, 45, 46, 48, 49
(see also program)
computer programmer, 14, **36**, 37,
40, 46 (see also programmer)
computer revolution, **40**
computer security, **38**
computer simulation, **28**, 34, 35, 45
computerspeak, **3**
computer system, **4**, 16, 32, 38, 42
computer-telephony, **41**
computer theft, **38**
computer virus, 38, **39**
computers, types of, 12-15
concertina fold paper, **11**
concurrent programming, **14**
configurations, **21**
connections (to the Internet), 42
connector, **17**
consumables, **11**
contact manager, **49**
continuous stationery, **11**
contrast button, **7**
control bus, **20**
control pad, **16**
control panel, 6, **15**
control unit (in a CPU), **9**
converter, AD (Analogue-Digital), **32**,
47
converter, DA (Digita-Analogue), **32**,
47
co-processor, 12
maths, **21**
copy (hard and soft) **10**
copying,
blocks, **26**
files, **25**

cordless mouse, **7**
core applications, **26**
core wars, **46**
corrupt disk, **38**
corrupting (a message), **18**
coupler, acoustic, **48**
cps (characters per second), **11**, 47
CPU (Central Processing Unit), 5, 8,
9, 12, 14, 20, 21, 47
CISC, **21**, 47
RISC, **21**, 47
user-removable, **12**
cracking (a password), **38**
crashed/crashing, **38**
crash testing, **29**
crime, computer, **38**
crop, **28**
crosstalk, **18**
CRT (Cathode Ray Tube) monitor, **7**,
13, 47
cursor, **7**
cursor control keys, **6**
customizable palette or toolbox, **28**
customized styles, **30**
custom-written software, **25**
cutting and pasting, **26**
cut sheet paper, **11**
cyan (in printing), **10**
cyber, **40**
cyberculture, **40**
cyberguru, **48**
cyberphobia, **40**
cyberskills, **40**
cybersociety, **40**
cyberspace, **42**, 44
cyberspeak, **3**
cyberzine, **46**

D

DA (Digital-Analog) converter, **32**, 47
daisy chain, **48**
daisywheel, **10**
daisywheel printer, **10**
DAP (Digital Audio Processing), **32**, 47
DARPANET (Defence Advanced
Research Progects Agency
NETwork), **42**, 47
DAT (Digital Audio Tape), **33**, 47
data, **4**
visual, **27**
DataBase Management System
(DBMS), **27**, 47
database software, **27**
database, multimedia, **27**
databank software, **27**
data bus, **20**
data capture, **31**
data cartridge, **23**
datacomms, **18**
datacommunications, **18**

data compression,19, **23**, 48, 49
data element, **14**
data entry worker, **14**
data file, **25**
dataglove, **34**
data hierarchy, **27**
data highway, **48**
data library, **14**
data lines, **17**
data packet, **42**
Data Processing (DP) department, **14**, 47
data protection, **38**
data wires, **17**
daughterboard, **8**
DBMS (DataBase Management System), **27**, 47
DCC (Digital Compact Cassette), **33**, 47
debugger, **37**
debug tool, **37**
decimal code, **44**
decode unit, **9**
decrypting, **38**
dedicated computer, **15**, 34
dedicated connection, **42**
dedicated key, **6**
dedicated word processor, 10, **15**
default, **48**
defining, **29**
defragging, **38**
defragmentation, **38**
degauss button, **7**
deleting, **25**, 46
deleting (in compositing), **31**
demodulate, **19**
density, 23
    double, **23**
    high, **23**
design, wire frame or wire mesh, **29**
designing (a program), **37**
design software, **28**, 29 (see also CAD)
desktop case, **12**
desktop metaphor, **24**
desktop modem, **19**
desktop PC, **4**, 13
DeskTop Publishing (DTP) software, **28**, 47
detachable lid, **13**
dial-in connection, **42**
dialogue, **24**
dialogue box, **24**
dial-up connection, **42**
dial-up modem, **19**
dictation software, **32**
digital, **4**, 19, 32, 33, 45
Digital-Analog (DA) converter, **32**, 47
Digital Audio Processing (DAP), **32**, 47
Digital Audio Tape (DAT), **33**, 47
digital camera, **17**
digital cartooning systems, **31**

digital community, **45**
Digital Compact Cassette (DCC), **33**, 47
Digital Compact Cassette player, 3, 33
digital generation, **40**
Digital Image Processing (DIP), **30**, 47
digital information, **20**
digital musical instrument, **33**
digital noise reduction system, **32**
digital revolution, **40**
digital rights, **48**
digital signal, **19**, 32
digital sound, **32**, 33
digital space, **24**
digital telephone line, **45**
digital video camera, 3, **17**
digital video clip, **35**
digitization, **4**
digitizer mouse, 3, **30**
digitizing tablet, **30**
DIP (Digital Image Processing), **30**, 47
direct debit card, **41**
Direct Neural Interface (DNI), **45**, 47
directory, **25**
    online, **42**
disc,
    compact, **23** (see also CD)
    erasable optical, **23**
    floptical, **23**
    magneto-optical, **23**
    optical, 3, **23**, 33
    Write Once Read Many (WORM), **23**
disc drive,
    compact, 5, 8, **35**
    optical, **23**
discussion group, **43**
disk, 5, 23, 38
    corrupt, **38**
    floppy, 3, 4, **23**, 25, 33, 38, 39
    hard, 4, **8**, 11, **23**, 25, 38, 49
    magnetic, **23**
disk cache, **23**
Disk Doctor, Norton Utilities, **39**
disk drive, 5, 12, 23, 24, 38, 48
    floppy, 5, 8, **23**
    hard, 8, **23**
disk drive lock, **38**
diskette, **23**
disk guard, 4, 23
disk hub, 4, 23
DNI (Direct Neural Interface), **45**, 47
docking station, **13**
document, 6, 14, **25**, 26, 43
documentation, **25**
    program, **37**
domain, **42**
dongle, 3, **38**
DOS, **24**, 26, 47 (see also MS-DOS)
dot matrix indicator, **6**
dot matrix printer, **10**

dots per inch (dpi), **11**
double clicking, **7**
double density, **23**
down, **38**
downloading, 11, **19**, 25, 43
downtime, equipment, **38**
DP (Data Processing) department, **14**, 47
dpi (dots per inch), **11**
drafting pens, **17**
draft quality, **11**
DRAM (Dynamic RAM), **22**, 47
drawing tools, **28**
drive, **23**
    Bernoulli, **48**
    disk, see disk drive
    CD/CD-ROM, 3, 8, **35**
    SCSI ("scuzzy"), **23**
    tape, 5, **23**, 49
drive (as a verb), **24**
drive bay, **8**, 9
driver, **24**
    printer, **10**
drum (in a drum scanner), **16**
drum (in a laser printer), **11**
drum kit, electronic, **33**
drum machine, **33**
drum scanner, **16**
DTP (DeskTop Publishing), **28**, 47
D-type flip-flop, **21**
dual batteries, **13**
dual scan LCD screen, **13**
duplex transmission, **19**
dweeb, **46**
Dynamic RAM (DRAM), **22**, 47

E

earthed mouse mat, **38**
eat up, **46**
Eckert, Presper, **44**
editing (in word processing), **26**
editing (sound), **32**
editor (in programming), **37**
edit out, **31**
edit tool, **28**
edu (in an email address), **42**
education, 34-35
edutainment, **34**
effects, sound, **33**
effects algorithm, **33**
EFTPOS (Electronic Funds Transfer at Point Of Sale) system, **15**, 41, 47
EISA (Extended ISA) bus, **20**, 47
electrical circuit, **8**
electricity, static, 7, 38
electro-acoustic music, **33**
electronic anarchy, **46**
electronic book, **35**
electronic diary, **13**

electronic drum kit, **33**
electronic etiquette, **19**
electronic guidance system, **15**
electronic keyboard (musical), **33**
electronic library, **40**
electronic mail, see email
electronic musical instrument, **33**
electronic outlaw, **38**
electronic piano, **33**
electronic rights, **48**
electronic terrorist, **38**
electronic typewriter, **15**
electrotransvestism, **46**
elegant programming, **37**
element (in finite element analysis), **29**
element, data, **14**
email/e-mail, 19, 24, 37, **42**, 46
email address, **42**
email header, **42**
emoticon, **43**
empty bucket, **22**
emulate, **12**
encoder, **7**
encrypting, **38**
end user, **4**, 14
enhance, **48**
enhancement software, **48**
ENIAC (Electronic Numeric Integrator And Calculator), 14, **44**, 47
ENTER key, **6**
entertainment, 34-35
entry, **27**
envelope, **42**
EPROM (Erasable Programmable ROM), **22**, 47
equipment downtime, **38**
erasable optical disc, **23**
Erasable Programmable ROM (EPROM), **22**, 47
erasing, **25**
ergonomic keyboard, 3, **39**
ergonomic mouse, **7**, 39
error, **9**
ethernet LAN, **18**
etiquette, electronic, **19**
everyday use of computers, 4, 15, 40
.exe (file extension), **25**
executable, **25**, 36
execution unit, **9**
expanding (RAM), **22**
expandable RAM, **12**
expansion bus, **20**
expansion card, **8**, 13, 19, 20, 22, 30, 32, 48
local bus, **20**
expansion slot, **8**, 20
extension, file, **25**
external modem, **19**
external port, **13**
external storage device, **23**
e-zine, **46**

F

facilities, Internet, **42**
facsimile machine, **19**
factory automation, **15**
failure, computer, 38
failure, systems, **38**
fanfold paper, **11**
fantasy game, **34**
FAQ (Frequently Asked Questions), **43**, 47
fax machine, **19**, 40
fax/modem, **19**
Fear, Uncertainty and Doubt (FUD) factor, **40**, 47
feature extraction, **16**
feed, **11**
feet (on a chip), **21**
feet, keyboard, **6**
Ferranti Mark I, **44**
fibre, optical, **18**
fibre optic cable, **18**
field, **27**
file, 10, 11, 19, 22, **25**, 26, 28, 42, 43, 49
data, **25**
program, **25**
text, **25**
voice, **32**
file extension, **25**
file manager, **25**
filename, **25**
File Processing System (FPS), **27**, 47
file server, **19**
file transfer protocol (ftp), **43**, 47
filleting function, **29**
fill function, **28**
filter (in graphics software), **30**
filter, anti-glare, **7**
filter function, **27**
financial analysis software, **27**
financial software, **27**
finite element analysis, **29**
fire button, **16**
firmware, **22**
fixed point arithmetic, **21**
flame mail, **43**
flame war, **43**
flaming, **43**
flatbed scanner, **16**
flight console, **16**
flight simulation, **34**, 35
flightstick, **16**
flight yoke, **16**
flip-flop, **21**
floating point arithmetic, **21**
floating point operation, **21**
FLoating point Operations Per Second (FLOPS), **21**, 47
flocking algorithm, **31**
floppies, **23**

floppy disk, 3, 4, **23**, 25, 33, 38, 39
floppy disk drive, 5, 8, **23**
FLOPS (FLoating point Operations Per Second), **21**, 47
floptical disc, **23**
flowchart, **37**
followup, **43**
fonts, 11, **26**
footer, **26**
footprint, **4**
near-zero, **48**
foot rest, **39**
"for Windows", **26**
form, **27**
format, **26**
formatting (a disk), **23**
formatting text, **26**
form feed, **11**
FORTRAN (FORmula TRANslation), **36**
four-colour printing, **10**
Fourth Generation Language (4GL), **36**
FPS (File Processing System), **27**, 47
fractal, **31**
fragmentation, hard disk, **38**
frame (in animation), **31**
frame, text, **28**
fraud, computer, **38**
freeware, **25**
freeze frame video, **17**
Frequently Asked Questions (FAQ), **43**, 47
ftp (file transfer protocol), **43**, 47
ftp site, **43**
FUD (Fear, Uncertainty and Doubt) factor, **40**, 47
full bucket, **22**
full-duplex modem, **19**
full motion video, **17**
full tower, **12**
fully upgradable, **12**
function, **4**, 10, 21, 24, 26, 28, 29, 38
aerial view, **29**
fill, **28**
filleting, **29**
filter, **27**
line, **28**
search, **27**
sort, **27**
trimming, **29**
functional electronic stimulus system, **41**
functionality, **4**
function key, **6**
fusing system, **11**
fuzzy logic, **45**
fuzzy set, **45**

G

game, computer, 3, 16, 25, 33, **34**, 35, 48

action, **34**
adventure, **34**
arcade, **34**
combat, **34**
fantasy, **34**
hack'n'slash, **34**
hand-held, 3, **34**
multi-user (dungeon), **48**
pocket, **34**
racing, **34**
role-playing, **34**
simulation, **34**
space combat, **34**
space war, **34**
sports, **34**
strategy, **34**
topographical, **34**
video, **34**
gameplay, **34**
gamer, **34**
games computer, 15, **34**
games console, **34**
games software, 25, **34** (see also
    game)
gate, logic, **21**
gate, noise, **32**
Gates, Bill, **44**
gateway, **42**
GB (gigabyte), **22**, 47
Gbyte, **22**
gear, VR, **34**
geek, **46**
general-purpose computer, **15**
generation (chips), **12**
generation, digital, **40**
Geographical Information Systems
    (GIS), 28, **48**
Gibson, William, **44**
gig, **22**
gigabyte (GB), **22**, 47
gigaflop, **21**
GIS (Geographical Information
    Systems), 28, **48**
glare, **7**
glitch, **48**
global change, **27**
global village, **45**
glove, VR, **34**
gopher, **43**, 46
gopherspace, **43**
gov (in an email address), **42**
grabbing, **31**
graph, **30**
Graphical User Interface (GUI), **24**, 47
graphics, computer, 5, 6, 7, 8, 10,
    11, 18, 19, 25, 28, **30**, 31,
    33, 34, 35, 39, 42
    analysis, **30**
    bitmapped, **30**
    character, **30**
    presentation, **30**

    real-time, **34**
    video, **30**
    video-quality, **34**
graphics adaptor, **7**
graphics card, **30**, 35
graphics pad, **30**
graphics software, 25, **30**, 31 (see
    also graphics)
graphics tablet, 3, **16**, 30
grey modem, **19**
greyscale screen, **5**
GUI (Graphical User Interface), **24**, 47
guided vehicle system, **15**
guide, **28**
gulp, **46**

H

hacker, 18, **38**, 46
hacking into, **38**
hack'n'slash game, **34**
half-duplex modem, **19**
halftone scan, **16**
hammer, **10**
hand-held computer game, 3, **34**
Hand-Held Computer Terminal
    (HHCT), **41**, 47
hand-held PC, **13**
hand scanner, **16**
handshaking, **19**
hand-shaped mouse, **39**
hang-up, **38**
hard automation, **15**
hard copy, **10**
hard disk, 4, 8, 11, **23**, 25, 38, 49
    removable, **38**
hard disk (as a name for the processing
    unit), **8**
hard disk drive, 8, **23**
hard disk fragmentation, **38**
hardware, 4, 8, 16, 18, 30, 35, 38, 49
hatching, **29**
header, **26**
header, email, **42**
head-mounted display, **34**
headphones, **35**
headset, VR, **34**, 45
heatsink, 8, **9**
help desk, **14**
HHCT (Hand-Held Computer
    Terminal), **41**, 47
hiding, **29**
high bandwidth, **19**
high density 3.5 inch disk, **23**
high-level programming language, **36**
high resolution, **7**
highway, data, **48**
holiday, virtual, **45**
home, computers at, 4, 40
home automation, **17**
home computer, **4**

home shopping, **41**
honourware, **25**
hook up, **42**
host (on a network), **19**
host (on the Internet), **42**
hot swap, **13**
housekeeping, **24**
housing, **21**
hypermedia, **35**
hypertext, **35**, 40, 43
hypertext-linked, **43**
hypertext novel, **40**
hypertext word, **35**
hyphenation, **26**

I

IBM (International Business
    Machines), 12, **44**, 47
IBM clone, **12**
IBM-compatible, **12**
IBM Personal Computer (IBM PC), 4,
    12, 20, 44
IC (Integrated Circuit), **21**, 47
icon, **24**, 26, 28
iconifying, **26**
identifier, **25**
image, **7**, 38
image processing, **30**
image quality, **11**
image scanner, **16**
Imagery, Computer-Generated (CGI),
    30, 47
immune, **39**
impact printer, **10**
implant, brain, **45**
importing, **28**
inbetweening, **31**
indicator, clock speed, 8, **9**
indicator, dot matrix, **6**
indicator, LED, **8**
Industry Standard Architecture (ISA)
    bus, **20**, 47
infected, **39**
Infobahn, **46**
infonaut, **46**
information, digital, **20**
information manager, personal, **49**
information section, **14**
information superhighway, **46**
Information Technology (IT), **40**, 47
Information Technology (IT)
    department, **14**
information technology revolution, **40**
infotainment, **34**
infotech revolution, **40**
ink cartridge, **10**
ink chamber, **10**
inkjet plotter, **17**
inkjet printer, 3, **10**, 17
input, 4, 14, 15

---

*Page numbers in bold type (eg **37**) show where to find the main explanation of a word or phrase.*   **55**

musical, **32**
pen-based, **13**
input (as a verb), **6**
input and output devices, **6**, 7, 8, 9, 13, 16
input device, **6**, 7, 8, 9, 13, 16
Input/Output port (I/O port), **8**
Input/Output System, Basic (BIOS), 8, **9**, 47
INSERT key, **6**
install, **25**
Institut de Recherche et de Coordination Acoustique/ Musique (IRCAM), **33**, 47
in-store touchscreen, **41**
Integrated Circuit (IC), **21**, 47
Integrated Services Digital Network (ISDN), 42, **45**, 47
integrated software, **25**
Intel, 9, **12**, 44
Intel 80486, **12**
Intel Inside, **12**
Intelligence, Artificial (AI), 36, **45**
Intellipoint, 24
intended virus, **39**
interact, **6**
interactive, **35**
interactive, Compact Disc- (CD-i), 47, **48**
interactive learning, **35**
interface, **8**, 19, 23
modem, **19**
Interface, Direct Neural (DNI), **45**, 47
Interface, Graphical User (GUI), **24**, 47
interface, natural language, **48**
Interface, Small Computer Systems (SCSI), **23**
Interface, User (UI), **24**
Interface Adaptor, Peripheral (PIA), **8**
interface unit, bus, **9**
interference, **17**, 18
static, **38**
internal modem, **19**
internal storage device, **23**
International Business Machines (IBM), 12, **44**, 47
internaut, **46**
Internet, 18, 19, 40, **42**, 43, 46, 47, 48, 49
Internet facilities, **42**
Internet Protocol (IP), **42**, 47
interpreter program, **36**
invisible effects, **48**
invoke, **48**
I/O port (Input/Output port), **8**
IP (Internet protocol), **42**, 47
IRCAM (Institut de Recherche et de Coordination Acoustique/ Musique), **33**, 47
ISA (Industry Standard Architecture) bus, **20**, 47

ISDN (Integrated Services Digital Network), 42, **45**, 47
ISDN (Integrated Services Digital Network) adaptor, 42, **45**
italic text, **26**
IT (Information Technology), **40**, 47
IT (Information Technology) department, **14**
IT instructor, **40**
IT trainer, **40**

J

JANET (Joint Academic NETwork), **47**
jargon, computer, **3**
Jerusalem virus, **39**
JK-type flip flop, **21**
job, **4**
Jobs, Steve, **44**
Joint Academic NETwork (JANET), **47**
joke virus, **39**
journey, virtual, **42**
joystick, 3, **16**, 34
Jughead, **43**
jukebox, medical, **27**
junking, **46**
justified text, **26**

K

K, **22**
KB (kilobyte), **22**
Kbyte, **22**
key, 4, **6**
alphanumeric, 6
CAPS LOCK, **6**
cursor control, **6**
dedicated, **6**
ENTER, **6**
function, **6**
INSERT, **6**
PAGE DOWN, **6**
PAGE UP, **6**
RETURN, **6**
SHIFT, **6**
soft, **49**
toggle, **6**
key (animation), **31**
keyboard, 4, 5, **6**, 12, 13, 24, 27, 38, 39, 43, 48
ergonomic, 3, **39**
touch-sensitive, **6**
keyboard, electronic (musical), **33**
keyboard cable, 5, 6
keyboard feet, **6**
keyboardist, **14**
keyboard port, **8**
keypad, 6, **27**
keystroke, **48**
killer application, **43**
kilobaud, **48**

kilobyte (KB), **22**
kit, **16**
multimedia, 16, **35**
knowledge-based project, **14**

L

label, **27**
LAN (Local Area Network), **18**, 42, 47
land, **23**
language,
problem-oriented, **36**
programming, **36**, 45
Language, COmmon Business Oriented (COBOL), **36**
Language, Fourth Generation (4GL), **36**
Language, Page Description (PDL), **11**
laptop, **13**
laser beam, **11**, 23
laser printer, 10, **11**
layer, **29**
layout, page, **26**
LCD (Liquid Crystal Display), 7, **13**, 47
LCD monitor/screen, 7, **13**
lead (cable), **17**
learning, **35**
leased line, **19**
LED (Light-Emitting Diode), **7**, 47
LED indicator, **8**
letter quality, **11**
library,
algorithm, **37**
data, **14**
electronic, **40**
program, **37**
virtual, **40**
lid, detachable, **13**
life, virtual, **45**
life cycle, **37**
light detector, **7**
Light-Emitting Diode (LED), **7**, 47
line,
data, **17**
digital telephone, **45**
leased, **19**
line feed, **11**
line function, **28**
line printer, **10**
line quality, **17**
lines, digital telephone, **45**
linked up, **18**
linker, **36**
Liquid Crystal Display (LCD), 7, **13**, 47
Lisp, **45**
list, mailing, **43**
listserv, **43**
literate, computer, **40**
live, **4**
liveware, **46**
loading, **22**, 25
Local Area Network (LAN), **18**, 42, 47

*Page numbers in bold type (eg **37**) show where to find the main explanation of a word or phrase.*

local bus, **20**
     PCI (Peripheral Component
          Interconnect), **20**, 47
     VESA (Video Electronics
          Standard Association),
          20, 47
local bus expansion card, **20**
local change, **27**
local server, **19**
location, memory, **22**
lock,
     case, **38**
     disk drive, **38**
lofting, **31**
logging in, **48**
logging off, **48**
logging on, **48**
logging out, **48**
logic,
     fuzzy, **45**
     program, **36**
logic bomb, **39**
logic gate, **21**
logic symbol, **21**
Logic Unit, Arithmetic (ALU), **9**, 47
logic-seeking print head, **11**
Logo, **36**
long-distance mouse, **16**
loop (cable), **18**
loop (program), **37**
loose tracking, **28**
loudspeaker, **8**
Lovelace, Ada Augusta, Countess, **44**
low-level programming language, **36**
low-rad/low-radiation monitor, **7**
low resolution, **7**
loyalty card, **41**
loyalty scheme, **41**
luggable, **13**
lunchbox, **46**
lurking, **46**

M

Mac (Apple Macintosh), 4, 9, **12**, 24,
     44
machine,
     drum, **33**
     facsimile/fax, **19**
     Turing, **44**
machine code, **36**
Mac, Power, **12**, 44
Macintosh, see Mac
macro, **48**
macro flowchart, **37**
magenta (in printing), **10**
magnetic disk, **23**
magnetic strip, **15**
magneto-optical disc, **23**
mail, **19**
     e-, **42**

electronic, **42**
flame, **43**
snail, **42**
mailbase, **48**
mailing list, **43**
mail-only connection, **42**
mainboard, **8**
mainframe, 4, **14**, 48
mains adaptor, **13**
maintenance, program, **37**
Maltese Amoeba virus, **39**
Management System, DataBase
     (DBMS), **27**, 47
manager,
     contact, **49**
     file, **25**
     personal information, **49**
Manchester University Mark I, **44**
manipulating, **28**
manual, **25**
margin, **26**
Mark I, Ferranti, **44**
Mark I, Manchester University, **44**
mark scanner, **16**
mask, **31**
mat, mouse, **5**
     anti-static, **38**
     earthed, **38**
     with wrist rest, 39
mat, scan, **16**
material properties, **29**
maths co-processor, **21**
matrix, **10**
matrix matching, **16**
Mauchly, John, **44**
maximize, **26**
MB (megabyte), **22**, 47
MByte, **22**
MCA (Micro Channel Architecture)
     bus, **20**, 47
meat, the, **46**
mechatronics, **48**
media, 40
medical expert system, **27**
medical jukebox, **27**
meg, **22**
megabyte (MB), **22**, 47
megaflop, **21**
megahertz, **9**
memory, 4, 9, 11, 12, 13, 20, **22**, 30
     cache, 12, **22**
Memory, Random-Access, see RAM
Memory, Read-Only, see ROM
memory buffer, **11**
memory card, **13**
memory location, **22**
Memory Modules, Single In-line
     (SIMMs), **22**, 47
menu, **24**
menu bar, **24**
menu-driven user interface, **24**

metaphor, desktop, **24**
Michelangelo virus, **39**
micro, **12**
Micro Channel Architecture (MCA)
     bus, **20**, 47
microchip, **21**
microcomputer, **12**
microfloppy, **23**
microphone, 35
microprocessor, **9**
Microsoft, 24, **44**
Microsoft Disk Operating System
     (MS-DOS), **24**, 44, 47
Microsoft Windows®, 24, **26**, 44
MIDI-compatible, **33**
MIDI recording software, **32**
MIDI socket, **33**
MIDI (Musical Instrument Digital
     Interface) system, **32**, 47
midi tower, **12**
Millions of Instructions Per Second
     (MIPS), **21**, 47
MIMD (Multiple Instruction Multiple
     Data) parallel processing, **14**
MIME (Multi-purpose Internet Mail
     Extensions), **42**, 47
minicomputer, **14**
minifloppy, **23**
minimize, **26**
mini tower, **12**
MIPS (Millions of Instructions Per
     Second), **21**, 47
mirror, virtual, **41**
mixing, **32**
mixing desk, **32**
model, **31**
model, acoustic, **32**
modelling, **29**
     physical, **31**
     polygonal, **31**
     spline-based, **31**
model space, **29**
modem (MOdulate/DEModulate), 3,
     13, 17, **19**, 42, 45, 48, 49
     BABT-approved, **19**
     desktop, **19**
     dial-up, **19**
     external, **19**
     fax/, **19**
     full-duplex, **19**
     grey, **19**
     half-duplex, **19**
     internal, 13, **19**
     portable, 13, **19**
     simplex, **49**
     V22bis, **49**
     V32bis, **49**
     Vfast, **49**
modem adaptor, **19**
modem card, **19**
modem interface, **19**

---

*Page numbers in bold type (eg **37**) show where to find the main explanation of a word or phrase.*

modulate, **19**
module, **37**
monitor 4, 5, **7**, 12, 28, 30, 49
    Cathode Ray Tube (CRT), **7**, 13, 47
    low-rad/low-radiation, **7**
    true colour, **49**
monochrome scan, **16**
monochrome screen, **5**
mono scan, **16**
morphing, **31**
Mosaic, **43**
motherboard, **8**
Motion Pictures Experts Group (MPEG) compression, 47, **48**
Motorola, **12**
mouse, 3, 5, **7**, 13, 16, 17, 24, 27, 30, 34, 35, 38, 39, 43, 46
    3-D, **34**
    ballpoint, **13**
    cordless, **7**
    digitizer, 3, **30**
    ergonomic, **7**, 39
    hand-shaped, **39**
    long-distance, **16**
    pen, **13**
    tail-less, **7**
    virtual, **34**
    VR, **34**
mouse ball, **7**
mouse button, 5, **7**
mouse cable, 5, 7, 16
mouse mat, **5**
    anti-static, **38**
    earthed, **38**
    with wrist rest, **39**
mouse pad, **5**
mouse port, **8**
mouse potato, **46**
moving (files), **25**
MPC (Multimedia Personal Computer), **35**
MPEG (Motion Pictures Experts Group) compression, 47, **48**
MS-DOS (Microsoft Disk Operating System), **24**, 44, 47
MUD (Multi-User Dungeon) game, **48**
multilayered 2-D animation, **31**
multimedia, 16, 23, **35**
multimedia author, **40**
multimedia bundle, 16, **35**
multimedia database, **27**
multimedia designer, **40**
multimedia kit, 16, **35**
Multimedia Personal Computer, (MPC), **35**
multimedia-prepared, **35**
multimedia-ready, **35**
multimedia software, 16, 23, **35**
multimedia system, **41**
Multiple Instruction Multiple Data

(MIMD) parallel processing, **14**
multiple users, **14**
multiplexed bus, **20**
multiplexing, time division, **20**
Multi-purpose Internet Mail Extensions (MIME), **42**, 47
multitasking, **14**, 24
Multi-User Dungeon (MUD) game, **48**
multi-user game, **48**
music, **33**
musical input, **32**
musical instrument,
    digital, **33**
    electronic, **33**
Musical Instrument Digital Interface (MIDI), **32**, 47
music software, 32, 33

N

nand gate, **21**
National Science Foundation NETwork (NSFNET), **42**, 47
natural language interface, **48**
navigating, **24**
Near Letter Quality (NLQ), **11**
near-zero footprint, **48**
nerd, computer, **46**
nest, **37**
net, **18**
net, neural, **45**
Net, the, **42**
net citizen, **46**
net cop, **46**
net cult, **46**
net evangelist, **46**
nethead, **46**
netiquette, **46**
netizen, **46**
net judge, **46**
netoisie, **46**
net server, **19**
net slang, **46**
netster, **46**
net surfing, **46**
net traffic, **46**
netter, **46**
net user, **46**
network, 11, 14, 15, 17, **18**, 19, 25, 39, 40, 41, 42, 45, 46, 47, 48, 49
network, neural, **45**
Network,
    Local Area, (LAN), **18**, 42, 47
    Total Area (TAN), **49**
    Wide Area, (WAN), **18**, 42, 47
networked, **18**, 25
Network News, **43**
netzine, **46**
Neural Interface, Direct, **45**, 47
neural net, **45**

neural network, **45**
Neuromancer, 44
newbie, **46**
newbie hunting, **46**
newsgroup, **43**, 46
newspaper, online, **40**
NiCad (Nickel Cadmium) battery, **13**
NiMH (Nickel Metal Hydride) battery, **13**
NLQ (Near Letter Quality), **11**
node, **18**
noise, **46**
noise reduction system, digital, **32**
non-impact printer, **10**
non-volatile, **22**
nor gate, **21**
Norton Utilities Disk Doctor, **39**
notebook, 4, **13**, 19
not gate, **21**
nozzle, **10**
NSFNET (National Science Foundation NETwork), **42**, 47
number crunching, **14**
numeric keypad, **6**
nybble, **46**

O

object, **48**
object code, **36**
Object-Oriented Programming (OOP), **48**
OCR (Optical Character Recognition) scanner, **16**, 47
on line, **4**, 18
online, **18**
online democracy, **49**
online directory, **42**
online media, **40**
online newspaper, **40**
online postings, **40**
online shopping, **41**
online tutorial, **49**
on/off switch, 5, 7, **8**
"on the Net", **42**
OOP (Object-Oriented Programming), **48**
opening (files), **25**
Operating System (OS), 22, **24**, 26, 44, 47
operations, **9**
    floating point, **21**
operations section, **14**
operator,
    computer, **14**
    systems, **49**
Optical Character Recognition (OCR) scanner, **16**, 47
optical disc, 3, **23**, 33
optical disc drive, **23**
optical fibre, **18**
optical LAN, **18**

---

*Page numbers in bold type (eg **37**) show where to find the main explanation of a word or phrase.*

org (in an email address), **42**
organizer, personal, **13**
or gate, **21**
OS (Operating System), 22, **24**, 26, 44, 47
OS/2, **24**
OS, Mac, **24**
outlet, **13**
outline, **11**
output, **4**, 10
output (as a verb), **6**
output device, **6**, 7, 8, 9, 10, 13, 16, 17

P

package, software, **25**
packet, **19**
    data, **42**
Packet Assembler and Disassembler (PAD), **19**, 47
pad,
    control, **16**
    graphics, **30**
    mouse, **5**
    pressure, **34**
    track, **16**
PAD (Packet Assembler and Disassembler), **19**, 47
page (in DTP), **28**
page (in RAM), **22**
page (in a videotex system), **27**
page, Web, **43**
Page Description Language (PDL), **11**
PAGE DOWN key, **6**
page layout, **26**
page printer, **10**
PAGE UP key, **6**
pages per minute (ppm), **11**, 47
paint effects package, **30**
paint package, **30**
paint palette, **30**
palette, **28**
    customizable, **28**
    paint, **30**
    user definable, **30**
palmtop, **13**
pan, **28**
paper, 10, 11
paperless media, **40**
parallel cable, **17**
parallel computing, **14**
parallel port, 8, **17**
parallel processing/processor, **14**
parallel programming, **14**
parallel transmission, **17**
parity, **49**
parking, **49**
Pascal, **36**
passive radiant tag, **41**
password, **18**, 37, 38

password protection, **18**
pasting, **26**
patch, software, **38**
pattern-matching, **32**
payment card, **41**
PC (Personal Computer), **4**, 6, 8, 9, **12**, 13, 17, 20, 22, 23, 24, 26, 32, 34, 47
    desktop, **4**, 13
    hand-held, **13**
    IBM, 4, **12**, 20, 44
    multimedia, **35**
    portable, **13**, 44
    Power, **12**, 44
PC 1211, Sharp, **44**
PCB (Printed Circuit Board), **8**, 47
PCI (Peripheral Component Interconnect) local bus, **20**, 47
PCMCIA (Personal Computer Memory Cards International Association) expansion card, **20**, 47
PDL (Page Description Language), **11**
pen-based input, **13**
pen mouse, **13**
pens, plotter, **17**
Pentium™ Processor, 9, **12**
peripheral, **16**, 17, 18
Peripheral Component Interconnect (PCI) local bus, **20**, 47
Peripheral Interface Adaptor (PIA), **8**
Personal Computer, **4**, **12**, 32, 34
    (see also PC)
Personal Computer Memory Cards International Association (PCMCIA) expansion card, **20**, 47
personal financial management software, **27**
personal information manager, **49**
personal organizer, **13**
petal, **10**
phase diffusion, **49**
phone, touchtone, **49**
photogrammetry, **31**
physical modelling, **31**
PIA (Peripheral Interface Adaptor), **8**
piano, electronic, **33**
picture element (pixel), **7**
piracy, software, **38**
pirating, **38**
pit, **23**
pixel, **7**, 30
PKware, **49**
PKzip software, **49**
place, **28**
platen, **10**
plotter, **17**
plotter pens, **17**
pocket computer game, **34**
point, **26**

"point-and-click" learning, **35**
pointer, 5, **7**, 13, 16, 24
    cell, **27**
point size, **26**
polygonal modelling, **31**
post, **43**
postings, online, **40**
port, **8**, 13, 17
    external, **13**
    I/O (Input/Output), **8**
    keyboard, **8**
    mouse, **8**
    parallel, 8, **17**
    printer, **17**
    RS-232, **17**
    serial, 8, **17**
portable modem, 13, **19**
portable PC, **13**, 44
PostScript, **11**
power down, **13**
power-hungry, **46**
Power Mac, **12**, 44
Power PC, **12**, 44
Power PC chip, **12**
power supply, **9**
    autosensing, **13**
ppm (pages per minute), **11**, 47
prefetch unit, **9**
presentation graphics, **30**
pressure pad, **34**
pressure-sensitive brush, **30**
pressure-sensitive stylus, **30**
primitives, **29**
print department, **14**
Printed Circuit Board (PCB), **8**, 47
printer, 5, **10**, 11, 17, 18, 24, 48
    black and white, **10**
    bubblejet, **10**
    built-in, **10**
    character, **10**
    colour, **10**
    colour thermal, **48**
    daisywheel, **10**
    dot matrix, **10**
    impact, **10**
    inkjet, 3, **10**, 17
    laser, 10, **11**
    line, **10**
    non-impact, **10**
    page, **10**
    serial, **10**
printer cable, 5, **10**
printer driver, **10**
printer paper, 10, 11
printer port, **17**
printer RAM, **11**
printer ribbon, **10**
printer roll, **11**
printer ROM, **11**
printer server, **11**
print head, **10**

---

*Page numbers in bold type (eg **37**) show where to find the main explanation of a word or phrase.*

logic-seeking, **11**
printing,
bi-directional, **11**
four-colour, **10**
three-colour, **10**
printing pins, **10**
printout, 6, **10**
print queue, **11**
print resolution, **10**
print server, **11**
print sharing, **11**
print spooler, **10**
problem-oriented language, **36**
problems, computer, 38-39
processing, **4**, 30, 32
audio, **32**
Digital Image (DIP), **30**
image, **30**
parallel, **14**
remote, **14**
processing power, **9**, 30, 46
processing speed, 12, **21**
processing unit, 4, 5, **8**, 9, 12, 14,
15, 16, 17, 18, 19, 23
central, see CPU
processor, **9**
co-, 12, **21**
parallel, **14**
Pentium™, 9, **12**
program, computer, 4, 10, 13, 14,
15, 16, 19, 23, 24, 25, 26,
27, 31, 32, 33, **36**, 37, 38,
39, 43, 44, 45, 46, 48, 49
program decomposition, **37**
program documentation, **37**
program file, **25**
program library, **37**
program logic, **36**
program maintenance, **37**
programmer, computer, 14, **36**, 37,
40, 46
programming, 6, 14, 32, 33, **36**, 37,
48
concurrent, **14**
elegant, **37**
object-oriented (OOP), **48**
parallel, **14**
top-down, **37**
programming language, **36**, 45
high-level, **36**
low-level, **36**
propeller head, **46**
protection test unit, **9**
protocol (on computer networks), **19**
protocol (on the Internet), **42**
file transfer, see ftp
pseudocode, **37**
public display, computerized, **6**
public domain, **49**
publisher, software, **36**
Publishing, DeskTop, see DTP

pull-down menu, **24**
pulse, **9**

Q

quality,
CD- (sound), **32**
draft, **11**
image, **11**
letter, **11**
line, **17**
Near Letter (NLQ), **11**
video- (graphics), **34**
Queeg virus, **39**
Questions, Frequently Asked, see
FAQ
QWERTY keyboard pattern, **6**

R

racing game, **34**
radiation, **7**
RAM (Random-Access Memory), 9,
11, 12, **22**, 24, 25, 30, 46, 47
Complementary Metal Oxide
Semiconductor (CMOS
RAM), **22**, 47
dynamic (DRAM), **22**, 47
expandable, **12**
printer, **11**
shadow, **22**
static, **22**
video (VRAM), **30**
virtual, **22**
RAM battery, **22**
RAM capacitor (in a notebook), **13**
RAM chip, 8, 12, 22
Random-Access Memory, see RAM
random-dot stereogram, **31**
range, **27**
ray tracing, **29**
reader, barcode, **6**
read from, **23**
Read-Only Memory, see ROM
read/write head, **23**
Reality, Virtual, see Virtual Reality
real-time (performance), **33**
real-time graphics, **34**
reboot, **8**
rec (newsgroup topic), **43**
recognition (software),
character, **13**
optical character, **16**
voice, **32**,
voice, speaker-independent, **49**
word, **32**
record, **27**
recording software, MIDI, **32**
Reduced Instruction Set Computer
(RISC) CPU, **21**, 47
refresh (LCD screen), **13**

refresh (RAM), **22**
registers, **9**
registration black, **10**
relationship, virtual, **46**
remote processing, **14**
removable hard disk, **38**
rendering, **29**
Repetitive Strain Injury (RSI), **39**, 47
reset button, 5, **8**
resistance testing, **29**
resistor, **9**
resizing, **28**
resolution,
high, **7**
low, **7**
print, **10**
resume, auto, **13**
retouching, **31**
RETURN key, **6**
reverse feed, **11**
ribbon, printer, **10**
rights, digital or electronic, **48**
RISC (Reduced Instruction Set
Computer) CPU, **21**, 47
robot, **15**, 17, 36, 40, 45, 49
robotic prosthetic, **49**
rodent (gopher), **46**
rodent (mouse), **46**
role-playing game, **34**
roller (in a mouse), **7**
roller (graphics brush), **30**
roll, printer, **11**
roll paper, **11**
ROM (Read-Only Memory), 9, 11, **22**,
47
CD-, 23, **35**, 40, 47
Erasable Programmable
(EPROM), **22**, 47
printer, **11**
ROM chip, 8, 22
rotating, **28**
rotoscoping, **31**
router, **49**
row, **27**
RS-232 port, **17**
RSI (Repetitive Strain Injury), **39**, 47
rule, **28**
ruler, **28**
run(ning), **24**, 36, 39
running, up and, **4**

S

safety equipment, 39
sample (sound), **32**, 33
satellite, communications, **18**
saving, 4, **22**, 24, 25
scan,
CAT (Computerized Axial
Tomography), **15**
colour, **16**

halftone, **16**
mono, **16**
monochrome, **16**
scan head, **16**
scan mat, **16**
scanner, **16**, 18
barcode, **6**, 41
CAT (Computerized Axial
Tomography), **15**, 47
drum, **16**
flatbed, **16**
hand, **16**
image, **16**
mark, **16**
Optical Character Recognition
(OCR), **16**, 47
scanner window, **16**
scanning in, **16**, 30
school, computers at, 4
sci (newsgroup topic), **43**
scientists, 4, 36, 45
screen, 5, 6, **7**, 13, 15, 16, 17, 24,
25, 26, 27, 32, 34, 35, 38,
39, 41
greyscale, **5**
colour, **5**
LCD, 7, **13**
monochrome, **5**
screen break, **39**
screen burn, **38**
screen saver, **38**
scrolling, **6**, 28
SCSI (Small Computer Systems
Interface), **23**, 47
SCSI ("scuzzy") drive, **23**
search and replace, **26**
search function, **27**
sector, **23**
security, computer, **38**
segment (of a program), **37**
segment (of RAM), **22**
selecting, **7**
self-scanning, **41**
semiconductor, **21**
sending, **10**
serial cable, **17**
serial port, 8, **17**
serial printer, **10**
serial transmission, **17**
server, **19**
file, **19**
local, **19**
net, **19**
print/printer, **11**
service provider, **42**
set, fuzzy, **45**
set (mathematical formula), **31**
shadow RAM, **22**
shareware, **25**
Sharp PC 1211, **44**
shield, **18**

SHIFT key, **6**
shopping, home/online/virtual, **41**
shouting, **46**
show-stopper, **46**
shrinkwrapped software, **25**
signals, analog and digital, **19**, 32
silicon chip, 3, **21**, 44
SIMD (Single Instruction Multiple
Data) parallel processing, **14**
SIMMs (Single In-line Memory
Modules), **22**, 47
simplex modem, **49**
simulation, computer, **28**, 34, 35, 45
flight, **34**, 35
simulation game, **34**
simulation training, **35**
\Single In-line Memory Modules
(SIMMs), **22**, 47
Single Instruction Multiple Data
(SIMD) parallel processing, **14**
site, ftp, **42**
size controls, **7**
skewing, **28**
skin, **31**
slang, **46**
SLOC (Source Lines Of Code), **37**, 47
slot, expansion, **8**, 20
Small Computer Systems Interface
(SCSI), **23**, 47
smart card, **41**
smileys/smilies, **43**
snail mail, **42**
snap-on trackball, **13**
snowflake LAN, **18**
soc (newsgroup topic), **43**
socket, 8
MIDI, **33**
Zero Insertion Force (ZIF), **12**
soft, **49**
soft boot, **49**
soft copy, **10**
soft key, **49**
software, **4**, 12, 14, 22, 23, **24**, 25,
26, 27, 28, 29, 30, 31, 32,
33, 34, 35, 36, 38, 42,
44, 46, 48, 49
applications, **24**
bundled, **25**
business, **27**
business accounting, **27**
Computer-Aided Design
(CAD), 15, 25, **29**, 30,
47
Computer-Aided Testing
(CAT), **29**, 47
custom-written, **25**
databank, **27**
database, **27**
design, **28**, 29
Desktop Publishing (DTP), **28**,
47

enhancement, **48**
financial, **27**
financial analysis, **27**
games, 25, **34**
graphics, 25, **30**, 31
integrated, **25**
MIDI recording, **32**
multimedia, 16, 23, **35**
personal financial
management, **27**
PKzip, **49**
shrinkwrapped, **25**
sound and music, **32**, 33
speech synthesis, **32**
systems, **24**, 36
utility, **24**
voice recognition, **32**
software designer, **36**
software development, **36**
software engineer, **36**
software house, **36**
software metrics, **37**
software package, **25**
software patch, **38**
software piracy, **38**
software publisher, **36**
Software Quality Assurance (SQA),
37, 47
software suite, **25**
software tools, **37**
sort function, **27**
sound, 6, 8, 18, **32**, 33, 35, 42
CD-quality, **32**
computer-generated, **32**
digital, **32**, 33
sound card, **32**, 35
8-bit, **32**
16-bit, **32**
sound effects, **33**
sound software, **32**, 33 (see also
sound)
sound wave, **32**
source code, **36**, 37
Source Lines Of Code (SLOC), **37**, 47
source program, **36**
space,
digital, **24**
model, **29**
virtual, **34**
space bar, **6**
space combat game, **34**
space war game, **34**
spamming, **46**
speaker, **35**
speaker-independent voice
recognition, **49**
spec, **12**
special interest group, **43**
special-purpose computer, **15**
specification, **12**
Spectrum, ZX, **12**

*Page numbers in bold type (eg **37**) show where to find the main explanation of a word or phrase.*

speech synthesis software, **32**
speed,
     clock, **9**
     processing, 12, **21**
spellcheck, **26**
splicing, **32**
spline-based modelling, **31**
spoofing, **38**
spooler, print, **10**
sports game, **34**
spread, **28**
spreadsheet, 13, **27**
sprite, **34**
sprocket, **11**
SQA (Software Quality Assurance), **37**, 47
standalone computer, **18**
standard passive LCD screen, **13**
star LAN, **18**
static electricity, 7, 38
static interference, **38**
static RAM, **22**
stereogram, random-dot, **31**
storage device, 4, **22**, 23, 24
strain injury, see RSI
strategy game, **34**
stretching, **28**
strip, magnetic, **15**
stylus, **30**
sub-directory, **25**
subdomain, **42**
sub-notebook, **13**
subtopic, **43**
supercomputer, **14**
superhighway, information, **46**
superhighwayman, **46**
Super Video Graphics Array (SVGA), **7**, 47
support service, user, **37**
support staff, **14**
surfing on the Net, **46**
suspend, auto, **13**
SVGA (Super Video Graphics Array), **7**, 47
symbol, logic, **21**
synthesizer, **33**
synthesizer chip, **32**
synthesizing, **32**
.sys (file extension), **25**
sysop, **49**
system,
     computer, **4**, 16, 32, 38, 42
     operating, 22, **24**, 26, 44, 47
System 6, **24**
System 7, **24**
System 7.5, **24**
systems analyst, **14**, 36
systems failure, **38**
systems operator, **49**
systems programmer, **36**
systems software, **24**, 36

systems unit, **8**

T

tab, **26**
tablet,
     digitizing, **30**
     graphics, 3, **16**, 30
tabulate, **26**
tagging system, **41**
tail, **7**
tail-less mouse, **7**
TAN (Total Area Network), **49**
tape cartridge, 14, **23**
tape deck, **23**
tape drive, 5, **23**, 49
tape streamer, **49**
tape transport, **23**
task, **4**
TCP/IP (Transmission Control Protocol/Internet Protocol), **42**, 47
techie, **46**
technical support staff, **14**
Technical Word Processor (TWP), **26**
technician, **14**
technobabble, **3**
technological warfare, **15**
technophobia, **40**
technospeak, **3**
telecentre, **40**
telecomms, **18**
telecommunications, **18**
telecommunications satellite, **18**
telecommuting, **40**
telecomputer, **45**
telecottage, **40**
teleport, **45**
telepresence, **49**
teleputer, **45**
telesurgery, **49**
teleworking, **40**
Telnet, **49**
template, **28**
tendinitis, **39**
tenosynovitis, **39**
terminal, **14**
terminal connection, **42**
tester, beta, **37**
testing, alpha, **37**
Testing, Computer-Aided (CAT), **29**, 47
text, **5**, 6, 10, 18, 26, 28
text box, **28**
text editor, **37**
text file, **25**
text formatting, **26**
text frame, **28**
text-to-voice system, **32**
texture mapping, **31**
text wrapping, **28**

TFT (Thin Film Transistor), **13**
the meat, **46**
thick (coaxial cable), **18**
thicknet, **18**
thin (coaxial cable), **18**
Thin Film Transistor (TFT), **13**
thinnet, **18**
three-colour printing, **10**
Three-Letter Acronym (TLA), **47**
throughput, **49**
thumball, **13**
ticket, computer-coded, **15**
tight tracking, **28**
time bomb, **39**
time division multiplexing, **20**
timesharing, **14**
TLA (Three-Letter Acronym), **47**
toggle key, **6**
token, **18**
token ring LAN, **18**
toner, **10**, 11
toner cartridge, **10**, 11
tool, **28**
     drawing, **28**
     edit, **28**
     software, **37**
toolbox, **28**, 30
top-down programming, **37**
topic, **43**
topographical game, **34**
topology, **18**
Total Area Network (TAN), **49**
touching up, **31**
touchscreen, **15**
     in-store, **41**
touch-sensitive keyboard, **6**
touchtone booking, **49**
touchtone phone, **49**
tower, **12**
track (electrical), **8**, 20
track (formatting), **23**
trackball, **13**
trackerball, **13**
tracking (in DTP), **28**
tracking (with a hand scanner), **16**
track pad, **16**
tractor, **11**
traffic, net, **46**
trainer, IT, **40**
transceiver, **18**
transistor, **21**, 44, 49
translation system, **49**
transmission, **17**
     parallel, **17**
     serial, **17**
Transmission Control Protocol/Internet Protocol (TCP/IP), **42**, 47
transputer, **49**
trashing (data), **39**
trimming function, **29**

Trojan/Trojan horse virus, **39**
true colour monitor, **49**
trunk, **48**
turbo button, 5, **8**
Turing, Alan, **44**
Turing machine, **44**
TV on demand, **40**
tweak, **37**
TWP (Technical Word Processor), **26**
.txt (file extension), **25**
type, **26**
typeface, 10, **26**
typewriter, electronic, **15**

U

UI (User Interface), **24**, 47
underlined text, **26**
Unique Product Code (UPC), **15**
UNIX, **24**
up and running, **4**
UPC (Unique Product Code), **15**
upgradability, **12**
upgradable, fully, **12**
upgrading, **12**
Usenet, **43**
user, **4**
user-definable brush, **30**
user-definable palette, **30**
user-friendly, **4**
User Interface (UI), **24**, 47
user-removable CPU, **12**
user support service, **37**
user-unfriendly, **4**
utility software, **24**

V

V22bis modem, **49**
V32bis modem, **49**
vaccine, **39**
value, **27**
valve, **49**
vapourware, **46**
VDU (Visual Display Unit), **7**, 47
Veronica, **43**
versions, **37**
VESA (Video Electronics Standard
      Association) local bus, **20**, 47
Vfast modem, **49**
VGA (Video Graphics Array), **7**, 47
Vic 20, **12**
video, freeze frame, **17**
video, full motion, **17**
video camera, digital, 3, **17**
video card, **30**
video CD, **40**
video CD player, **40**
video clip, digital, **35**
video compositing, **31**
video conferencing, **17**

Video Electronics Standard
      Association (VESA) local bus,
      20, 47
video game, **34**
video graphics, **30**
Video Graphics Array (VGA), **7**, 47
video on demand, **40**
videophone, **41**
video-quality graphics, **34**
Video Random-Access Memory
      (VRAM), **30**
video-telephony, **41**
videotex system, **27**
view, **28**
virtual catalogue, **41**
virtual experience, **45**
virtual holiday, **45**
virtual journey, **42**
virtual library, **40**
virtual life, **45**
virtual mirror, **41**
virtual mouse, **34**
virtual RAM, **22**
Virtual Reality (VR), 29, **34**, 45, 47
virtual relationship, **46**
virtual shopping, **41**
virtual space, **34**
virtual travel system, **45**
virtual world, **34**
virus, computer, 38, **39**
virus-writer, **39**
vision systems, **15**
visual data, **27**
Visual Display Unit (VDU), **7**, 47
visualizing, **29**
visuals (for ambient music), **33**
VL-bus (VESA local bus), **20**
voice command, **32**
voice-controlled word processor, **32**
voice file, **32**
voice-input system, **32**
voice recognition software, **32**
volatile, **22**
VR (Virtual Reality), 29, **34**, 45, 47
VRAM (Video Random-Access
      Memory), **30**
VR gear, **34**
VR glove, **34**
VR headset, **34**, 45
VR mouse, **34**

W

wafer, **21**
WAIS (Wide Area Information Service),
      47
WAN (Wide Area Network), **18**, 42, 47
warfare, technological, **15**
wave, sound, **32**
wave table, **32**
Web, the, **43**

Web browser, **43**
Web page, **43**
wetware, **46**
What You See Is What You Get
      (WYSIWYG), **26**, 47
Wide Area Information Service (WAIS),
      47
Wide Area Network (WAN), **18**, 42, 47
wild card, **49**
WIMP (Windows, Icons, Mouse and
      Pointer) interface, **24**
window, 26
window, scanner, **16**
Windows®, see Microsoft Windows®
Windows 95, **44**
Windows, Icons, Mouse and Pointer
      (WIMP) interface, **24**
wire frame design, **29**
wire mesh design, **29**
wired (on a network), **18**
wired (slang), **46**
wizziwig, see WYSIWYG
word, **21**
word count, **26**
Word Processing (WP), **26**, 37, 47
word processor,
      dedicated, 10, **15**
      voice-controlled, **32**
word recognition software, **32**
word wrap, **26**
workgroup, **19**
work-on-the-go portable, **13**
worksheet, **27**
workstation, **15**, 24
World Wide Web (WWW), **43**, 47
worm (virus), **39**
WORM (Write Once Read Many) disc,
      23
Wozniak, Steve, **44**
WP (Word Processing), **26**, 37, 47
wrapping, text, **28**
wrist rest, **39**
Write Once Read Many (WORM) disc,
      23
write to, **23**
WWW (World Wide Web), **43**, 47
WYSIWYG (What You See Is What
      You Get), **26**, 47

Y

yellow (in printing), **10**

Z

Zero Insertion Force (ZIF) socket, **12**
ZIF (Zero Insertion Force) socket, **12**
zooming, **28**
Zuse, Konrad, **44**
ZX81, **12**
ZX Spectrum, **12**

---

*Page numbers in bold type (eg **37**) show where to find the main explanation of a word or phrase.*

The publishers are grateful to the following organizations and individuals for permission to reproduce material:

Cover: (Apple Mac computer) Apple Computer UK Ltd.
Contents page: (Combat game - "Cyclones", Space game - "Commander Blood") Mindscape International Ltd; (MIDI recording software) Cubase software by STEINBERG; (Computer-generated map) ERDAS (UK) Ltd; (Paint package graphics of skittles) SOFTIMAGE; (Ambient music graphics) Visuals from the Future Sound of London album "Lifeforms" courtesy of Virgin Records; (Computer-Aided Design image of car) Volkswagen.
p3: (Ergonomic keyboard) "Natural keyboard" © Microsoft Ltd; (CD-ROM drive) AZTECH UK Ltd; (Digital compact cassette player, Optical disc) PHILIPS; (Dongle) Software Security; (Inkjet printer) Canon (UK) Ltd; (Digital Video Camera) Computers Unlimited; (Modem) U.S. Robotics, Ltd; (Hand-held computer game) Systema; (Clip-on trackball) Watford Electronics Ltd; (Graphics tablet) c-star Software.
p10: (Inkjet printer, Colour printer) Canon (UK) Ltd; (HP Laserjet laser printer) HEWLETT-PACKARD COMPANY.
p12: (Apple Mac computer, Apple Computer logo) Apple Computer UK Ltd.
p13: (Notebook PC, Clip-on trackball) Watford Electronics Ltd; (Personal organizer) Canon (UK) Ltd; (Personal organizer with pen-based input) Sharp Electronics UK Ltd.
p14: (Charles Babbage) © Dr Jeremy Burgess/Science Photo Library.
p15: (Microwave oven) Whirlpool UK; (Dedicated Word Processor) Canon (UK) Ltd; (CAT scan of hand) © Robert Chase/Science Photo Library.
p16: (Long-distance mouse) Propoint remote pointing device available from LTS; (Graphics tablet) c-star Software.
p17: (Digital video camera) Computers Unlimited; (Plotter) HEWLETT-PACKARD COMPANY.
p18: (Fibre-optic cable) © Adam Hart-Davis/Science Photo Library.
p19: (Desktop modem, Modem card) U.S. Robotics, Ltd.
p21: (Close-up of chip's surface) © David Scharf/Science Photo Library.
p24: (Icons) © Microsoft Ltd.
p25: (Games software) Europress Software Ltd; (Graphics software) Reproduced using RenderWare® courtesy of Criterion Software Ltd; (Computer-Aided Design software) Image produced in Autosketch for Autodesk, © Autodesk Ltd.
p26: (Microsoft Windows logo) © Microsoft Ltd.
p27: (Business software users) © Tim Brown/Tony Stone Worldwide Photolibrary; (Prof. Meg Abyte) Reproduced by kind permission of Non Figg.
p28: (Computer-generated map) ERDAS (UK) Ltd.
p29: (CAD wire frame and rendered jet, CAD engine parts, CAD building) Images produced in Autosketch for Autodesk, © Autodesk Ltd; (Virtual Reality garage) Virtual Reality product range, Superscape (Virtual Reality software).

p30: (Paint package graphics of hangar and skittles) SOFTIMAGE; (Paint effects software - transparencies showing graphics) Flame Editing Interface, Discreet Logic (UK) Ltd.
p31: (Fractal computer art) © Dr Fred Espenak/Science Photo Library; (Inbetweening graphics) Discreet Logic (UK) Ltd; (Animated monster) SOFTIMAGE.
p32: (MIDI recording software) Cubase software by STEINBERG; (Scientist analyzing word patterns) © Hank Morgan/Science Photo Library; (Woman using DragonDictate voice recognition software) Dragon Systems UK Ltd.
p33: (Electronic keyboard) Yamaha-Kemble Music (UK) Ltd; (Electronic drum kit) Roland UK Ltd; (Ambient music graphics) Visuals from the Future Sound of London album "Lifeforms" courtesy of Virgin Records; (Digital compact cassette player) PHILIPS.
p34: (Hand-held computer game) Systema; (Combat game - "Cyclones", Space game - "Commander Blood") Mindscape International Ltd; (Racing game - "The Need for Speed") Electronic Arts; (Virtual reality user wearing VR gear) © James King-Holmes/W Industries/Science Photo Library.
p35: (Multimedia PC) Western Systems; (CD-ROM screens) Main Image Ltd; (Concept 90 Flight Simulator) Thomson Training & Simulation.
p38: (Earthed mouse mat) DAHLE (Anti-static Mat); (Disk drive lock) IDS; (Dongle) Software Security.
p39: (Disk Doctor graphic) Reproduced with the permission of SYMANTEC and Sentrybox. Usborne Publishing Ltd will respect all Symantec Corporation's copyrights. (Hand affected by carpal tunnel syndrome) © Custom Medical Stock Photo/Science Photo Library; (Ergonomic keyboard) "Natural keyboard" © Microsoft Ltd; (Mouse mat with built-in wrist rest) Acco-Rexel; (Hand-shaped mouse) Gem Distribution.
p40: (Child using computer) © David Young Wolff/Tony Stone Images; (Animatronic robotic dinosaur) The Natural History Museum, London; (Woman telecommuting) © David Hanover/Tony Stone Images.
p41: (Smart card used as reference) with thanks to London Transport Buses BEST project; (Photo of Andrew Walker using functional electronic stimulus system) Reproduced by kind permission of Andrew Walker and ASPIRE (Association for Spinal Injury, Research, Rehabilitation and Reintegration), with thanks to Fiona Barr; (Hand-held computer terminal) Remanco Systems Limited.
p42: (Computer network connections on the NSFNET) © NCSA, University of Illinois/Science Photo Library.
p43: (Marsupial frog) © Dr Morley Read/Science Photo Library; ("Veronica" from the Archie comics) Archie characters TM & © 1995 Archie Comic Publications, INC.
p44: (Ada Lovelace) MARY EVANS PICTURE LIBRARY; (William Gibson) Penguin Books Ltd.
p45: ("Manny" Android) © US Department of Energy/Science Photo Library; (Virtual Reality brain imaging) © Peter Menzel/Science Photo Library.

The publishers would like to thank Apple Computer Ltd, IBM UK Ltd, Intel Corporation UK Ltd, Microsoft UK Ltd, and Dan Jones (composer) for their help. Microsoft and Microsoft Windows are registered trademarks of Microsoft Corporation in the US and other countries.